IRRESISTIBLE

IRRESISTIBLE

LIZ BANKES

WALKER BOOKS
AN IMPRINT OF BLOOMSBURY
NEW YORK   LONDON   NEW DELHI   SYDNEY

First published in Great Britain in 2013 by Piccadilly Press Ltd.
E-book edition published in the United States of America in February 2013
by Walker Books for Young Readers, an imprint of Bloomsbury Publishing, Inc.
Hardcover edition published in April 2014
www.bloomsbury.com

Bloomsbury is a registered trademark of Bloomsbury Publishing Plc

For information about permission to reproduce selections from this book, write to
Permissions, Walker BFYR, 1385 Broadway, New York, New York 10018
Bloomsbury books may be purchased for business or promotional use. For
information on bulk purchases please contact Macmillan Corporate and Premium
Sales Department at specialmarkets@macmillan.com

Library of Congress Cataloging-in-Publication Data
Bankes, Liz.
Irresistible / Liz Bankes.
pages   cm
Originally published as an e-book by Piccadilly Press, 2012.
Summary: A steamy romance about a girl's passionate summer with the bad boy of
her dreams.
ISBN 978-0-8027-3621-5 (hardcover) • ISBN 978-0-8027-3622-2 (e-book)
[1. Love—Fiction. 2. Sex—Fiction.] I. Title.
PZ7.B22555Ir 2013   [Fic]—dc23   2012050748

Printed and bound in the U.S.A. by Thomson-Shore Inc., Dexter, Michigan
2 4 6 8 10 9 7 5 3 1

All papers used by Bloomsbury Publishing, Inc., are natural, recyclable products
made from wood grown in well-managed forests. The manufacturing processes
conform to the environmental regulations of the country of origin.

To Ryan, Tilly, and Billie
Best housemates ever

IRRESISTIBLE

Jamie Elliot-Fox is toxic.

I wrote that in my diary in the middle of last summer.
To warn myself. In case I got sucked in.
In case I let myself fall for it.
In case I unleashed a whole load of trouble.
But I still did.

Chapter 1

"Mia," she says, pronouncing it to rhyme with "higher."

I think about correcting her, but then I chicken out. It's fine. I'll just have a new name.

"Does that denote an exotic heritage?" she continues.

"Um, no. Well, Mom's part Welsh."

"Shame. We're trying to fill our minority quotas."

She watches me while I try desperately to think of something to say, then puts her hand over her mouth and mock-whispers, "I'm joking."

"Oh, okay!" I am able to breathe again. "I think my name was Dad's idea. He thought it sounded different. He wrote a song about it or something. I'll ask him the next time he visits. They were, like, seventeen when I was born," I try to explain.

She makes a small, polite cough that is definitely not polite.

I'm sure I've blown the interview. They probably

don't let you wait tables somewhere like this if you start off by talking about your parents' scandalous teenage pregnancy.

The woman looks down at her pad and then up again, as if she is erasing the past few minutes from her brain. She's sitting on an ornate wooden chair in front of a massive window. There are shadows over her face; her white teeth and shining eyes poke through the darkness, making her more frightening. She would be beautiful, I think, if she weren't so terrifying. Her blond hair is scraped back into a bun, and her eyebrows have been plucked into severe arches. When she looks up, she has a wide-eyed smile that looks more like the grimace of someone about to kill you.

"So, Mia, tell me a bit about yourself."

"I've just finished Year Eleven."

"That makes you...?"

"Sixteen."

"So I am assuming you have qualifications."

"Well, yeah, I've done all my GCSE exams. I mean, everyone in my year did. So . . . yes."

"I lose touch with these things—at James's and Dezzie's schools they do the International Baccalaureate. More rigorous, they say, don't they?"

I nod. Always best to nod.

"And what subjects did you take?"

"The ones you have to do, plus history, drama, and French. I also took a course in food tech."

She's looking at me like I'm speaking in Chinese. "Food tech might help prepare you for our restaurant, I suppose."

"Yes . . . Well, we mostly designed egg cartons, but I can

4

cook things. My mom taught me her version of spaghetti with meat sauce. Basically you just add a lot of wine."

I stop and think of the menu I saw when I was waiting in reception. "I mean, probably not the kind of wine you have here. Mom usually has a box of wine in the fridge, but you...probably...don't."

I'm doing that thing where I'm nervous and babble till I'm out of words. At least I didn't mention the time my chili chicken kebabs made my stepdad, Jeff, violently sick because I didn't turn the oven on correctly and the chicken was raw.

She smiles unkindly. "No." She lets the moment linger. "But French...That may be useful. We have an international clientele."

Hmm, I think. Useful if they want me to tell them what I did on my vacation or to describe the contents of my pencil case.

"Well, why don't I tell you a bit about Radleigh?"

She launches into a guidebook-style intro, which I start nodding along to. I mean, I did google the place. It has its own Wikipedia page, which talks about how Radleigh Castle has always been a hub for the rich and famous. It began as one of those authentic castles with knights and damsels and stuff. Then it was more of a grand stately home, inhabited by generations of dukes, before it was turned into a hotel at the beginning of the twentieth century. There's a hilarious part about how, a few centuries ago, there was some club for "mischief" based here, which got a reputation for "lewdness" with rumors of unmarried women becoming "excited," but that's all stopped now. I am not surprised. The guests here look pretty old. I expect they spend less time being lewd and more time falling asleep in the middle of the day.

Radleigh's Great Hall Restaurant is apparently famous for its "olde English" cuisine. That makes me think of pigs on spits with apples in their mouths. The restaurant is where I'll be working if I get this job. I wonder if I would get free food.

This woman is on the Wikipedia page too. Julia Elliot-Fox. She inherited the castle and then married a banker named Richard, and they have two kids: James, who's eighteen, and Desdemona, who's thirteen.

Julia is just getting to the nineteenth century when I look up to the window behind her.

There is a boy standing there. Watching me.

He's wearing a shirt with the collar turned up and shorts. There's a cigarette hanging from his mouth and an expensive-looking bottle in his hand. He's got messy hair, a bit of stubble, and lips that make him look like he's permanently pouting. At the same time that I'm wondering why he's staring at me, I notice that I can't seem to look away. He's only slightly to the side of Julia, so I can look right at him while she's talking.

It's his expression. He looks like he's smiling at some private joke. And his dark eyes seem to go right into my thoughts.

I force my gaze back to Julia, who is saying something about the war. I nod in a way that hopefully says, "I am very interested in the things you are saying," but my eyes flick back to the window.

The boy's eyes are stern, like he's examining me, but he still has the smile at the corners of his mouth. It looks like he's about to mouth something at me when someone else appears in the window. It's a girl, wearing a white shirt and black skirt;

6

I think she must work here, except enough of the buttons on her shirt are undone that you can see her bra, which is probably not part of the dress code.

She reaches out and puts her hand under his shirt to where the waistband of his shorts must be. He leans forward and kisses her.

And he's still looking at me.

Her hands run over his chest, while his stay by his sides, still holding the cigarette and the bottle.

They move up against the window. He must be pressed right against her, and I suddenly wonder what the weight of his body would feel like. I wonder how kissing him would taste and imagine his stubble grazing my neck.

I take a sharp breath in and force my eyes away from the window. Why on earth am I thinking things like that? I don't even know who the boy is. My hands, placed rigidly on my knees, suddenly feel hot, and I realize my mouth is dry. I've totally stopped nodding along to Julia.

The boy stops kissing the girl and takes a swig from the bottle. It has a dusty brown label. He hands her the bottle and kisses her on the nose, looking at me one more time. Then he reaches up and knocks twice on the window. He pats the girl on the butt, and then he's gone.

Julia stops midflow and coolly turns her head to the window. The girl looks terrified and stumbles back, almost dropping the bottle in the process.

Although I can't see her face, I can see that Julia gives a small shake of the head. She turns back to me and raises her eyebrows.

"Now. Tell me why you want to work at Radleigh Castle."

Chapter 2

The next ten minutes feel like ten years as I stutter and um my way through the interview. I don't tell her how I've been daydreaming about saving up lots of money and not going back to school in September, perhaps arranging an internship somewhere instead, or just traveling around and coming back when I've spent all my money.

I want to do things like end up on a mountain somewhere at five in the morning and see a huge lake stretching for miles with absolutely no one else around, or wander around a city, trying street food and meeting people who take me to some random music festival or beach party with a bonfire—basically, doing the things I can't do around here, the same town I've lived in for sixteen years.

Julia asks how I would handle the less-glamorous tasks, like cleaning the bathrooms. I pause. Mom's not the neatest of people, especially when she's had her book group (which is actually more of a wine and cackling group) over and gives me £10 to clean up. And Jeff has an office that is essentially a mountain of paper and cups of congealed tea. Matthew is only seven, so he's got an excuse for leaving a trail of candy wrappers and books behind him. Technically I'm the cleanest person in my house, but I don't know if that qualifies me to handle the Radleigh Castle restrooms. I tell her I like cleaning toilets. She doesn't say anything to that and just moves on to the next question, probably because my answer sounds pretty weird.

Finally, she asks me how I would deal with speaking to distinguished personages. I panic and say, "Curtsy at them?"

She says, "Well, I think we'll end there," and stands up.

As she walks me out, all I can think is, *Oh God, now I'll have to be like Lizzie from school and take a job working for the fish man.*

The interview room is just up the corridor from the main entrance, and we walk back over creaking floorboards, past paintings of people in wigs. A dark wooden door at the end of the corridor looks like it leads to a cellar or secret passageway or something. I think how this would have been an awesome place to grow up. Because Jeff is a history teacher, we've been on lots of family trips to old houses and castles. I went through a stage where I was obsessed with ghosts and would deliberately lose Mom, Jeff, and Matthew in order to find the quietest, spookiest room I could, and then I'd stand there, waiting for ghosts to come and scare me. I'd read stories about "real life hauntings" and had been convinced that every creak or whistle I'd heard was the "gray lady" or "mad monk" finally appearing.

I'm the same with movies and stuff—I start off desperately

hoping to be scared, but it never seems real enough. Gabi, my best friend, never had this problem; at sleepovers she would continually dig her fingernails into my leg when we were watching some slasher film we were probably too young for, while I was usually a little bored. And when we got taken to see *The Woman in Black* on the Year Eight theater trip, she got taken out for screaming too hysterically.

I think that if I get this job, I'll probably be here till late each night. My ten-year-old self would be delighted. Gabi's current sixteen-year-old self would go completely crazy. I'm going to look tonight for any scary "haunting" stories about this place. I bet there have been a few scary children singing nursery rhymes. Or maybe one of these portrait women in wigs was driven mad with grief and can still be heard wailing in the corridors.

We turn off into a room on the right, which is the reception area, where the receptionist had made me wait for ten minutes while she "verified" that I was really here for an interview, as opposed to being here to steal or set fire to things.

Julia asks the receptionist for "Jennifer Fish's mother's number."

"Unfortunately, we'll be letting her go," she explains.

"Oh? Why's that?" asks the receptionist, barely containing her desire to get the gossip.

"Overindulgence," Julia replies through her false smile. "And there'll be a bottle of port to replace."

The receptionist *tsk*s and mutters something under her breath that sounds like "Another one..."

Julia leaves to make her phone call and I sit opposite the receptionist. Jeff won't be here to pick me up for another half hour. I could probably walk, but I'm not totally sure of the way. I lean back, wondering what I'm going to do for half an hour, and the wooden back of the chair creaks loudly. I sit up quickly, thinking that breaking antique furniture is probably not the best way to fill my time.

The receptionist coughs. "We have books if you are looking for something to do, dear," she says pointedly. She's reading a book, exaggeratedly licking her finger each time she turns the page and peering at me over her glasses.

I look around. There's a shelf of very old-looking books behind me—the kind with brown leather spines. I wonder what she would do if I picked one up and did what she is doing, which is essentially wiping her spit all over it.

I'm about to pull out one of the old books when she snaps her fingers and points to a box by the door. It's full of paperbacks, mostly those with photo-style illustrations of couples kissing on the front. The one I choose has a guy with long hair and an oiled chest and a woman whose clothes are falling off. I wonder if they were left by guests and the receptionist has hoarded them. Well, at least it will pass the time.

After spending a while trying not to laugh at "dangerously sexy Dante" and his "rock-hard thighs," I feel a breeze coming from the door. I shift forward on my chair so I can see through an archway and into the castle courtyard.

Julia comes sweeping back in and sees me watching. "Do have a look around while you wait," she says.

I hand the receptionist back the book and thank her. She holds it in an overly dainty manner between her thumb and finger and places it back in the box.

I go across the corridor and into the courtyard. It's like a mini garden, with trees and flower beds and a stone path running through it. Walls loom at me on all sides, with windows too small to see into, apart from the ones at ground level. On the right I can see into the restaurant. The wall ahead of me is broken into a series of archways at the bottom that lead out to a terrace of stone slabs with tables and chairs on it. There's one old man at a table with his head on his chest, snoring. The restaurant leads to a conservatory building on the left, and through the glass I can see the outdoor swimming pool. Julia said it is available to guests in the day. Maybe staff get to use it in the evening . . .

It looks awesome, surrounded by stone pillars with plants growing around them. And at the end there's a building that looks like a Greek temple with four huge stone pillars at the front of it. I cannot believe people actually live here.

Sitting between the building and the pool on a lounge chair is the boy from the window. He's reading a book and smoking, putting the cigarette in his mouth each time he turns the page. He's wearing the same black shorts, but no shirt now. He's too far away to see clearly. I think that it would be useful in situations like these if I carried binoculars with me, then realize that makes me sound like a pervert. He's probably been swimming, I think. I imagine his chest drying off in the sun. Then my phone goes off loudly.

The old man snorts and glares around, and the boy looks up from his book. I fumble to reach the phone in my bag and run back through one of the arches into the courtyard. My phone is still blaring, and I still can't find it in my bag.

I press the answer button just as I reach the reception area again, and the receptionist is saying, "Excuse me . . ." above the noise of my ringtone.

On the phone, Jeff says, "I'm here! I think . . ."

I go out the old wooden door at the bottom of the left tower and walk across the gravel, heading to the parking lot on the left. I can't see Jeff's car, which is a relief, to be honest, because it's a Volvo and really old, and Gabi always says I should get him to park around the corner when he picks us up from parties. I tell him I'll start walking to meet him.

"I'm on a windy country lane. I nearly killed a deer!" he says helpfully.

I walk toward the point where the parking lot meets the lane and see Julia and another woman standing by a car. Julia is talking while the woman looks uncomfortable and fiddles with her car keys. As I pass them, I hear Julia say, "...a bottle of the nineteen-forty-five Graham's she'd stolen from the cellar. It won't be drinkable now that she's opened it and shaken it up."

"Mmm, yes. Of course. Shaken up," says the woman in a shrill, wobbly voice. "I'm very, very sorry. We'll replace the port, of course."

"I wouldn't worry," says Julia, and I know she'll be smiling the fake smile, "unless you have a thousand pounds to spare. It's not something one gets in the grocery store."

"David's a chartered accountant," the shrill woman says, and then trails off.

I'm nearly on the other side of the car before I feel I can turn and look. In the passenger seat is the girl I saw kissing the boy at the window. Even from here I can see a dark red stain at the top of her white shirt where she must have spilled the port. Pretty incriminating. She is crying, and on one side of her face her mascara has run down in a long black drip.

I wonder if I should tell them it wasn't her fault. Or even that if she did steal the port to drink with the boy, then it's his fault too. I hover behind them, but I can't speak up. Julia is too terrifying. And what if I didn't see everything? The girl in the car must be wondering what I'm doing. I try to give her a friendly smile, but I don't think she really registers me. She's looking back up at the castle.

The boy is standing at the front door with his hands in the pockets of his shorts. The huge stone facade towers behind him at a slight angle. At first I think he's too far away to have noticed us, but then I see his head turn in our direction, and for a second I'm sure that he's looking over at me. He lights up another cigarette and walks off.

Chapter 3

"O. M. F. G.," says Gabi, with a dramatic hand wave between each letter. She grips my arm across the table, nearly knocking my coffee over in the process.

"What?"

"Jamie. Elliot. Fox."

"Can you speak in normal sentences?"

"He's, like, famous, Mia."

"He seems like a jerk. What's he famous for?"

"Um, for being *rich* and *hot*? You must have heard about him! God, it's like you live under a bridge."

Within a second she's whipped out her phone and is scrolling rapidly. She hands it to me triumphantly. "Ta-da!"

A few people who are quietly murmuring over their coffee look at our table, which is something that often happens when we're out together. It's like Gabi has a volume dial on her voicebox that is always turned a few notches higher than everyone else's.

"That was some quick stalking, even for you," I tell her.

"But you want to see him, don't you?"

"No. Maybe. Okay, yes, I want to see him."

I'd like to be all nonchalant and cool, but I'm intrigued. Obviously he's good looking, with his stubble and dark eyes. And his muscly chest that I haven't actually seen close up, but that I imagine being muscly. Not that I've been imagining him walking around in just his shorts, all wet from the swimming pool.

But he clearly knows he's hot or he wouldn't go around kissing people in windows. Or staring. Why would he stare at me? What does he think I'm going to do—run outside and say, "Now that you've glared at me through a window, I must have you"?

Gabi sees that I've gone into a daydream, so she does her usual trick of digging her nail into my hand.

"Hey! Okay, so his Facebook is, like, really private, but Han and me met him and his friends that night we went to York's."

She says the night we went to York's. She means the night we didn't get into York's and instead stood freezing our asses off in a nearby bus shelter, passing around a Smirnoff Ice. It seems that these days it's all about trying to get into clubs and places, instead of just going to people's houses when their parents are away. I miss getting all excited about house parties and making playlists for them and putting all our money together to give to whichever tall person was going to go try to buy drinks at the supermarket. I have no chance of getting into any clubs—I'm only just over five feet tall, so bouncers spot me immediately. Gabi has the most enormous

16

boobs ever to have grown on a person, though, so she just strolls in.

Maybe if I get this job then I'll be able to socialize in the Radleigh Castle bar, like a sophisticated...um, woman, and drink port with Jamie Elliot-Fox. And kiss Jamie Elliot-Fox against windows. But without getting fired.

While Gabi's talking about that night, I look at the first picture. There's Jamie in a suit, but with the shirt collar open. He's leaning back on a sofa, casually holding a glass of wine, while the people around him, including two girls practically sitting on his lap, clutch vodka bottles and generally look totally wasted. He's fixing the camera with that same critical, amused look he had at the window.

"You took off with those goths," she continues.

Gabi thinks that anyone who doesn't like pop music is a goth. Actually Han's sister and her friends had turned up and were on their way to see a band, so I went with them.

"They're not—" I try to interrupt.

"Whatev. So you went with the goths and then I texted you saying we'd met all those Woodbridge guys outside the club and gone to their house party—remember?"

"Yeah, they were all named Tarquin or Octavian or something."

"So Jamie was there, and that was the night I became Facebook friends with that guy Willem."

"William?"

"No, *Willem*."

"That's not a real name."

Gabi dramatically takes a sip of her hot chocolate . Well, to anyone else it would be dramatic, but it's how she does everything.

"Anyway, Max got really jealous and they were, like, actually going to fight, but Fat Steve calmed everything down."

"Really?" I raise my eyebrows at her. "Max has never been in a fight, Gabs. We've never even seen a fight."

"Whatev. You weren't there. There was fighting in their *eyes*, Mia."

"Just not in reality."

"Exactly!"

"So you've met him, then?" I scroll through some more photos. He's not in all of them, but every so often he'll appear. On the beach in his shorts again, wearing shades. In another suit, sitting by a bonfire. In most of the photos he's got a drink in his hand, but he looks in control, in stark contrast to lots of the people around him.

"Well, he didn't talk much. He stood there drinking and watching everyone. Oh yeah, and he was with this girl, apparently. The richest girl I've *ever* seen. Like a horse with lots of hair. But all these other girls kept crowding around him, and he was whispering to them and making them laugh, like, really flirty. If Max did that, I'd go crazy. He said something to this one girl, and she took her top off and swung it around her head. Next thing, she's looking around for him, but he'd walked off!"

"Wow, he sounds great."

"His friends said he lives in this pool house outside Radleigh Castle. How awesome is that? He has parties all the time. When you work there, we should totally go— Babe!"

We are interrupted by Max's arrival.

"Hey, princess," he says, pointing both fingers at Gabi. He shuffles over in his ridiculously baggy jeans, stopping briefly when the oversized cap he wears perched on the back

18

of his head falls off. I'd like to point out that he is both white and middle class. Considering the amount Gabi bitches about other people's fashion sense, I think that she must go temporarily blind whenever Max is around.

He slides into our booth. "Aight, baby?"

Okay, make that temporarily blind and deaf.

Max nods at me. "Mia."

"Hi, Max."

Then he and Gabi start kissing, which, as is usual for them, carries on for about five minutes. I keep my eyes on her phone. A girl with dark curly hair keeps appearing in the photos; she must be the one Gabi was talking about, because she does have a *lot* of hair and is near to Jamie in most of the pictures. Her name is Cleo Farah. She is stunning, with big brown eyes, sharp cheekbones, and coffee-colored skin.

Max and Gabi are still firmly attached to each other's mouths, so I look at the next photo. Jamie is dressed up again, but it looks like it's for a family thing rather than a party. Maybe a wedding. He's wearing a vest and has his arm around a girl who looks about twelve years old. She must be his sister. He's smiling, but not in the frowny way he is in the other photos— this looks more real.

I suddenly realize how stalkerish this is and put Gabi's phone down.

At that moment, my own phone starts vibrating in the bag on my lap. I'd turned the sound off after the ringtone nearly gave me a heart attack at Radleigh Castle. It's a call from a private number.

The receptionist at Radleigh called me from a private number to arrange the interview. Maybe they're calling to say I got the job. Or that I didn't. Or that I was seen watching

19

Jamie in the swimming pool. There aren't laws against watching men in shorts—are there?

I realize I've just been staring at the phone and haven't actually answered.

"Mia, it's Julia Elliot-Fox. We'd like to offer you a waitress position."

Chapter 4

"This," says Julia, "is the wine cellar."

We shuffle toward the room, four pairs of feet crunching on the gritty stone floor.

"You are not to go in there."

We stop.

"Johan, our sommelier, has the key, and he will send you up what you need in the dumbwaiter behind the bar."

I realize there is a man with a white mustache in the room, who has just taken a bottle from one of the shelves and is noting something down on a pad. He looks at us haughtily and then returns to his work.

Julia closes the door and walks back past us, her heels echoing in the corridor. We follow her up some steps and through a door that leads outside again. We come out at the rear of the castle, near the kitchens and the restaurant, with the swimming pool just visible.

The boy next to me taps my shoulder and whispers, "Which is worse, Johan or a pile of dog poo?"

"What?" I ask.

"Johan," the boy continues. "He's sommelier."

I look at him, confused. Does he not like sommeliers? Maybe he's just odd.

"Smellier," he explains.

It's so awful, it makes me laugh. "That is actually the worst joke I've ever heard."

"Oh, come on. I thought of it on the spot!"

"All right," I say. "Next time, maybe you should prepare a few in advance."

"Sorry, what was your name again?" he says. "I was focused on remembering which way the forks go in the silver service and didn't listen to anything else."

"Mia." I glance over at Julia to see if it's safe to talk. She's talking to one of the other waiters through the window. "You're Dan, right?"

"I am. You win on names, then." He nods toward Julia. "I hope there's not a test at the end of this tour; I'll be fed to the hounds." As he says it, he leans closer to me and grins, like we're sharing a secret.

I recognize Dan. He's two years ahead of me at the boys' school across the road from my school. I've never spoken to him before, though. He's got a really wide smile and dimples in his cheeks, and he keeps flicking his head to get his hair out of his eyes. I suddenly feel really pleased that I'm going to be working with him all summer.

"This is crazy, isn't it?" he says. "Imagine living here."

"We should," I tell him. "We could claim squatters' rights."

"Dibs on the west wing."

"I'll have the pool house." I smile. We've forgotten to keep our voices down.

"Will you?" Someone has come out of the door behind us, and I nearly jump out of my skin. Jamie raises his eyebrows at me as he walks past. Today he's wearing a black polo shirt with the collar turned up, which, with a feeling of stalkerish shame, I recognize from one of the photos.

I see Dan fiddle with the collar of his white waiter's shirt as we both watch Jamie head in the direction of the pool house. My stomach dips in embarrassment, and I can feel my cheeks burning. I instinctively smooth down my skirt. I went shopping with Mom and got this high-waisted skirt and fitted shirt and new black heels. Up until now I'd felt pretty good in my new clothes, as if looking all sharp and professional would help me not make a mess of everything.

I don't know why it's bothering me so much that Jamie just heard me. I probably won't even see him that often if he's off in his pool house all the time. I look up and catch Dan's eye, and he grins. I immediately feel more relaxed.

"And that," says Julia pointedly, making us both turn back to her, "is about everything. The more experienced staff will guide you. Melanie, I'd like you behind the bar tonight," she says to the older girl with us. She has long red hair and freckles and has been nodding a lot and saying "Hmm" during the orientation, as if she knows it all already. "Mia, you'll be on tables, and Daniel, you'll be in the kitchen."

"Just my luck," says Dan.

I feel slightly panicky. I'll be the most on display. I breathe out slowly. It will be fine. I practiced holding three plates at a time in Gabi's room, with her pretending to be a distinguished Radleigh diner. She got a bit too into it, throwing imaginary food across the room and shouting, "GARBAGE! UTTER DISGRACE!"

Melanie pipes up. "Julia?"

"Mrs. Elliot-Fox will do, I think," corrects Julia.

"Mrs. Elliot-Fox . . . sorry. I was just wondering, where should I put my engagement ring?" She holds up her hand with the ring facing out. "Simon would be so sad if anything happened to it, and—"

"I'll take it," cuts in Julia. "Although I don't know how you expect to damage it serving drinks. And do something about your hair, please."

"Oh, yeah, um, okay." Melanie holds out the ring and starts piling her hair into a ponytail. "Oh, I don't think I have a—oh dear . . ."

"I've got one," I say, handing her the spare hair tie from my wrist.

"To the kitchen!" says Dan.

As we follow him through the restaurant to start the shift, I run through all the things I need to remember. Serve food on the diner's left. Don't let them see you holding up your hands in L shapes to figure out which side left is. Don't fall over.

I'm completely exhausted. I didn't have a minute's break the whole night. Nonresidents have to book ahead, and residents are supposed to tell you when they are eating, but they all came in at different times, so there was constantly an order to take, food or a tray of drinks to bring over, or plates to clear. The kitchen was like a sauna whenever I had to go in, so I felt bad for Dan, who was there all night loading and unloading the dishwasher. He was looking pretty sweaty and crazy-eyed by the end. And when the guests had gone, there was the cleaning to do. When I offered to do the bathrooms at the end of the night, I thought Melanie was going to kiss me. It was tactical, really; all the windows are open in the restrooms, so it's much cooler in there. Job done, I suddenly hear the murmur of lots of voices outside, punctuated frequently by laughter and shouting. I think for a minute that people have gone into the dining room again, but then I hear splashing and realize the sounds must be coming from the pool. Closing time doesn't apply to them, then.

Back in the kitchen, Dan opens the fire door to let some air in and we sit on the step. "Jesus." He grins, wiping some dish-detergent bubbles from his hair. "Easing us in slowly, weren't they?"

"Argh!" I reply, leaning my head against the door frame.

"How were the fine diners?" he asks.

"Okay. Mostly they just ignored me, or pointed to their glasses when they wanted a refill. One old guy eating on his own said I was pretty."

"He must have been really drunk."

"Hey!" I elbow him in the leg.

"I'm kidding. You look lovely. I love my women dripping with sweat."

"Ha! Oh God, even laughing hurts." I shut my eyes. "I think I need to get up or I'll end up sleeping out here among the Dumpsters."

Dan stands up and pulls me to my feet. His arm tenses as it takes my weight, and I notice he's very muscly. When

I stand up, I'm close to him, even though I'm about a foot shorter. His hair falls across his face and he smiles at me. I realize I'm staring at him and go to fix my own hair, which had been gradually falling out of its clip all night.

"It looks good . . . all messy," he says.

One of the other waitresses calls over that she's locking up the kitchen.

"Okay," we both say together and then laugh. We've arranged to walk home across the park together, once Melanie's beloved Simon arrives to pick her up. I think she's probably been talking about beloved Simon for a lot of the night, because the other bartender looked like she wanted to kill her.

I tell Dan I'm just going to check the schedule so I know when to come in tomorrow. It's kept under the bar. I scan the sheet, and it takes a while for my brain to focus. I think I'm not on there for a moment and then I realize it's done by last name. Dan must be named Dan David, as it says *David* was in the kitchen tonight.

"And which one are you?"

Jamie's face is right over my shoulder. He seems to like sneaking up on people and generally being annoying. I can't help but notice he smells really nice. A sort of fresh, appley, spicy smell. I point at my name.

"Joseph," he says. "That's a pretty name."

"That's my last name. I'm Mia Joseph. Mia." I'm trying to sound serious and like he's bothering me, but I slip into a laugh at the end.

He raises his eyebrows. "Great. Well, Joseph, we're having a little party in there." He nods in the direction of the pool house. "And we're playing a little game." He cocks

26

his head to the side, still frowning at me with those full lips of his. He probably does that pouting thing on purpose.

"Okay. Well, have fun."

His presence is making me nervous. And sort of excited.

"A drink before you go home?"

I slide the schedule back under the bar. I wonder what would happen if I did stay. Part of me is aching to find out. Another, more sensible, part is telling me that the evidence so far suggests that a drink with Jamie would be a bad idea.

"Um, no, thanks. Dan's walking back with me, so . . ."

Jamie shrugs. "I don't know who Dan is."

Dan and Melanie look over from one of the tables. Dan's got a sort of a pleading look on his face. Melanie's probably showing him the pictures on her phone of her and Simon in Turkey.

"Oh, he's . . ."

I turn back, but Jamie has already gone.

Chapter 5

As we leave, Dan yawns. "I'm pretty tempted to take them up on the offer of a bed, to be honest."

Julia had told us that we were welcome to stay in the old servants' quarters on nights when we finished late. Apparently special events, particularly weddings, can go on into the early hours.

Dan widens his eyes, trying to make himself more awake. "Maybe not on the first night. We'll never leave!"

"We should one night, though—we can explore all those secret passages," I say and stop, slightly worried that I sound like the woman whose clothes were falling off on the cover of the receptionist's book. "The corridors," I clarify firmly. "That Julia told us about."

"Yeah, definitely," says Dan, looking amused. "On Friday it's the same as tonight for the late shift. Sleepover? You, me, and Melanie?"

We look at each other, both clearly thinking of beloved Simon. "Maybe not," we say in unison. Dan raises his eyebrows at me and we share a smile. It's the second time tonight we've said the same thing at the same time. We walk out the reception door and in front of the castle toward the grounds. It's surprisingly chilly for a summer evening, and though I try to hide it, I suddenly have an uncontrollable shiver spasm. Dan sees and insists I borrow his hoodie. I explain it's my own fault for bringing only a cardigan. I don't want to leave him cold.

Dan smiles and points out that the chilliness isn't actually that surprising, unless I was under the impression that Kent is part of the Mediterranean. I refuse again, until he reveals that he's brought a spare hoodie.

"Do you always carry spare clothes for handing out to women?"

"No! My mom just follows me around, putting things in my bag. I can also provide you with tissues, an apple, and a selection of plastic bags."

"Well, if we ever get lost somewhere, it's good to know we'll be able to share an apple and cry."

Dan laughs, and it sort of echoes around us. I turn around and look back at the castle. We're walking along the wide, central path that leads from the castle through the grounds. Only a few windows are lit up, so the black edges of the building seem to blur into the sky, making it look even more huge. I can still just about make out the two front turrets.

By the time we are out of sight of the castle and have found where the grounds meet the river, it is pitch black. It hadn't occurred to me that there wouldn't be any lights. I didn't technically tell Mom I was walking home. Jeff said he'd get me, but I said I was getting a lift. I suppose by a little stretch of the truth, I am. Dan *could* be carrying me.

Just as I have that thought, we have a sort of collision. His foot goes in front of mine and I trip. My hands flail in the air and grab the nearest solid thing, which turns out to be his face.

"Oh God! I'm sorry. I just grabbed your face!"

"It was mostly my ear. It's fine. I've got another one. Sorry I tripped you!"

"I don't think we really thought about this walking-through-darkness thing," I say, secretly glad that it's hiding my face. I have this thing that whenever the slightest embarrassment happens, I go bright red. Not in the attractive English-rose way; in the way that someone might glance over and say, "Oh, how strange. A tomato with the body of a girl."

We soon get into town and can finally see where we're going. I like walking along the main street when it's all empty, walking down the middle of the road because we can. It's so easy to talk to Dan, and we just flow from subject to subject, finding out more and more about each other. Dan just finished Year Thirteen and is taking a gap year off. He got into university for engineering, but he wants to go traveling first.

I immediately start asking him where he'd go and what he'd do, and he laughs in surprise. He says he wants to travel around Europe and then go to Ecuador and work on a farm. I tell him I want to see Barcelona. And Asia. And New Zealand.

"Planning your gap year already?"

"Yeah," I say vaguely, and drift off into a daydream in which I turn up at the station with my own rail pass and say, "Surprise, I'm coming too!" Dan, of course, is overjoyed and grabs my hands and says in an atrocious French accent, "*Paree, allons-y!*"

"Would you go on your own?" Dan says, and I'm jolted back to my less exciting life of not going to Paris and being slightly red.

I try to look at him like I'm a normal person and I didn't just invent an imaginary relationship for us. "I'd like to, but every time I bring it up, my stepdad goes on about how if I delay university, the tuition will probably go up again, and Mom says it doesn't sound very safe and that maybe I should go with my weird cousin Hugh. I would actually rather eat my own hand."

"Does she call him your 'weird cousin Hugh'?"

"No, but I said, 'Mom, he's weird' and she said, 'I know.' He got caught putting some of my LEGOS up his butt when we were little. And when he came to visit last year, he really freaked out my friend Gabi. We took him to a party and he got really drunk and licked her leg."

I'm completely rambling now. We've stopped walking because we've reached the end of my road and are just standing there chatting with our hands deep in the pockets of our hoodies and occasionally shivering. Dan looks down at his chest and frowns, like he's debating something. Then he looks up at me quizzically from behind his hair.

"You know, if I stay out there and end up living somewhere awesome, like New Zealand or something, you can always look me up. I'll be a traveling maestro by then."

"Well, yeah, I would probably need tissues and an apple at some point," I tell him.

He grins. "Exactly."

We both look around us, still hovering on the same spot. I don't really want to go inside, and I'm hoping he doesn't want to leave yet either. He scuffs his shoe back and forth on the ground, and I'm playing with the strings on the hoodie. Our eyes meet and then we both go, "So..." and then start laughing because this synchronicity is becoming ridiculous. He says we should probably swap numbers if we'll be working together all summer, so we do. As I'm typing in his name, I get a text from Mom asking when I'll be back. I tell Dan that I should go. He says he should probably get a few hours' sleep, as he's on the early shift tomorrow.

We look at each other for a moment, both unsure if we should hug at this point. But we just say "Bye" at the same time and then walk in opposite directions along the road.

I can't stop smiling to myself and must look insane. But it all seems so easy. Not like with Kieran, where Gabi and I plotted forever to get his number and there was a huge operation to get us alone in a room together at someone's party. Even when we were going out I had to be careful not to text too much so he didn't think I was clingy.

I freeze. Dan went to the same school as Kieran. He'd have been in the year above him, but still—he might have heard something. I have the usual crazy reaction I get whenever I think of Kieran—that I should just never speak to anyone who knows him or any of his friends. Obviously, that's impossible. I close my eyes and take a deep breath as panic washes over me again. It's always lurking somewhere in my mind, just to give me something to worry about. Or relive.

My phone is still in my hand after taking Dan's number and it vibrates, making me jump. It won't be Dan already, will it? I smile. If it is, at least I won't need to worry about seeming eager.

I look down, but it's not Dan. It's from a number I don't know. I open the phone, curious.

`Joseph, shame you couldn't stay.`

OH MY GOD! *He texted me.*

My heart lurches. The nervous, excited feeling I got when he was talking to me is pounding through me again.

The more sensible part of me notes that he must have gone and found my number somewhere, and that is pretty creepy behavior. I'll delete the text.

But maybe I'll save the number.

I mean, I might need it for...work.

Chapter 6

The next day I'm on the evening shift again, but Dan's on in the daytime. It must have been pretty difficult for him to get up early after the late night; I slept in till eleven. Jeff bobbed awkwardly into my room a little later and asked me if doing all these shifts would leave enough time for studying. I am supposed to be starting my A-Level exams to see what universities I'll qualify for in September. Well, assuming I've passed my GCSEs. I've picked my four subjects but have done absolutely no reading. In reply to Jeff I just said, "Hmm" and looked like I was doing something important and school related.

Gabi comes by in the afternoon before I have to leave, and I tell her about Dan and the number. Her reaction is typical Gabi.

"Thank GOD. I was beginning to think you were asexual."

I throw a magazine at her. "Oh, thanks!"

There's a pause, and I think about bringing up the Jamie text too, but she continues.

"Well, we know you weren't always asexual; but I thought after Kieran..."

I give her a look.

"Don't let him upset you still, Mi. He's a dick and a jerk." She grabs my arm to make her point. "A total jerk."

"Yep," I say abruptly.

She's always saying I should be more open and willing to talk about sex. Which is easy for her to say, seeing as she's doing it and I'm not. Gabi likes to show me all the positions she and Max do it in to "get me used to it" while I try to ignore her. Jeff walked in on her doing that once and he spluttered and spilled his tea everywhere. She said she was doing yoga, but I'm fairly sure he only pretended to believe her. He's definitely learned to knock before coming into my room now.

"So, this Danny..."

"Dan."

"Yeah. We need a *plan of action* to get you and this Danny up against the dishwasher."

"We do not," I tell her, although the brief mental image I get has some appeal.

Right on cue, I get a text. From Dan. He says the lunchtime shift is crazy and he has to stay to finish washing the pots, so we'll probably overlap.

"Overlap...," says Gabi, and wriggles her eyebrows up and down.

I ignore her.

"Say back, 'You can wash *my* pots...'"

35

"Probably not," I tell her, racking my brain for some sort of hilariously witty reply.

"Say back—"

"Shut up."

Gabi shuts up. For a tenth of a second. Then she starts reeling off more inappropriate things I could say. Most of them aren't even innuendo—just outright rude. But they're pretty funny. It's fun having a new person to get excited about. But I think most of all I've just got a good feeling about the summer. Having something to do and meeting new people. And getting one step closer to my secret traveling plan.

The first person I see when I walk into the restaurant isn't Dan. It's Jamie. He's sitting at the bar. I walk past and he doesn't look up at me, but he says, "Joseph," as I walk behind him.

"He's been here all day," says Dan as I get to the kitchen door, "trying to get Melanie to request different wines from downstairs for him. Then when she mentioned her wedding, he said, 'Oh, do tell me more,' so she started going on about it. It only took thirty seconds before he said, 'God, you're boring,' which shut her right up."

"Harsh," I say.

Suzy, the other barmaid, walks past us. "I don't know; if I have to listen to another Simon story, I will stick pins in my eyes. Or hers."

"Well, at least you're saying it about her and not *to* her," says Dan.

Suzy just narrows her eyes and says, "Hmm."

"Doesn't Julia mind him hanging around here all day?"

I say, still staring at him. He's doing that frowning and pouting thing.

"Whenever she's around, he chats to the guests," says Dan. "I heard one woman tell Julia how charming he is. It's only when she's gone that he starts bothering us."

Jamie is leaning across the bar now and whispering in Melanie's ear. Although she's determined to look serious, her cheeks turn pink and her eyes flicker as if she's flustered. As I watch his lips move, I think back to him appearing at the window on my interview day. I wonder if he's going to kiss her.

Dan whispers in my ear, "You're gaping."

I turn around and laugh. "Who says 'gaping'?"

He grins. "You should know, Gapy."

Dan hangs around for about half an hour of my shift. I realize after he's gone that he's taped a note to the fridge. He's drawn a cartoon woman with bulging eyes and a wide-open mouth and underneath has written, *Gapy McGape*.

I fold it up and put it in my pocket. Okay, Dan. Bring it on.

Chapter 7

The next day Dan and I are both on late shifts. At the beginning of the shift, I hide a cartoon I drew of a gaping cat for him to find in the cupboard where all the cleaning stuff is kept. A little later, when I'm taking the order from a family at table four, I find that he's drawn a gaping old lady on my order notepad. Thankfully, the family just thinks that I find the mom ordering sea bass very funny.

Later on, the other waiter, Andreas, suggests playing a game where we have to get as many song lyrics as possible into conversations with the guests. Suzy is up for it, but Melanie just gives us a pitying look.

I manage to get one in when someone orders moussaka and I pretend to mishear it. "Hey Macarena?" I ask them.

At the bar, Suzy has it easier because every time she makes a drink, she can say something like, "Oh, I call this one the 'Rude Boy,'" although it does sound odd when she's just talking about a glass of beer.

Toward the end of the shift there's just Dan and me left, and we're laughing at Andreas stopping in the middle of taking someone's order, clutching his chest and saying, "Oh, sorry, I think I've had A Total Eclipse of the Heart. Wait— actually, I'm okay."

"Speaking of desserts," says Dan, "do you want any of the pie before I throw it out?"

"Hmm, let me see." I lean over to the pie, scoop up some of the cream, and throw it at his forehead.

"Hey!" he shouts, and flings some back at me. It hits me in the eye. I try to throw it back at him, but he starts running around the central oven. Still unable to open one eye, I chase him and grab his arm, and he wriggles out of my grasp saying, "Beware Squinty the Cream Bandit," through his laughter.

The kitchen door bangs open and we freeze.

"We'd like some service, please."

"Oh, sorry, man. We've stopped making food," says Dan. I attempt to subtly de-cream my eye.

"I'm sure you can rustle something up." Jamie frowns at me. "Sometime tonight would be good." The kitchen door bangs shut again after him.

"Can we rustle something up?" I turn to Dan. I hope it turns out he is a gourmet food whiz. If it falls to me, we'll be serving them Mom's winey spaghetti or maybe just food poisoning.

Dan is rummaging in the fridge and finds a bowl of strawberry jelly.

He looks at me solemnly. "Do you think they're ready for this jelly?"

I head out into the restaurant with my notepad. Jamie is sitting at a table with a boy with black wavy hair and a red-faced, middle-aged man in a dinner jacket.

"What can I get you?" I say. "The chef's gone home, so our menu might be a little limited, but we'll do our best."

"You have something in your hair, Joseph," Jamie says with a look of amusement.

I go bright red and get the stray glop of cream from my hair.

He turns to his friend with the wavy hair. "Next shift, I will arrange to have her washed. What are we having?"

The temptation to tell him he's a dickhead and can get his own food is a big one. I clench my teeth together and just think of the money I'm earning.

The middle-aged man says, "Forget the food; I'll have more wine," and then laughs a throaty laugh that quickly turns into a cough. He turns purple. I watch him warily, wondering if I should do something about the fact that he could be choking to death. But as I move toward him, Jamie slaps him hard on the back and he stops.

"Freddie?" Jamie says to the other boy.

"Oh, ahm, oh, ay dain't know," he drawls.

I resist the urge to lean in closer and make it clear that I'm struggling to understand him through his accent. "Do you do, ahm, chaisy frites?" he asks.

"'Chaisy frites'?" I repeat. "Oh, cheesy fries! Yes, well, I'll see what we can do." It seems I might not need Dan to be a gourmet chef after all.

"Grait!" He grins, showing a lot of teeth.

"Make that two," says Jamie and gives me a big grin. "So kind of you."

40

Despite my mood, I smile back at him.

I set Dan to work on the fries. I figure it's probably okay if I get a bottle of wine from the bar. I'm not old enough to serve there, but the waiters are always grabbing drinks to take over to the tables when it's busy. As I look for the corkscrew, I see that Jamie has walked over and is leaning on the bar.

"Mr. Grassingham is our Parliament rep. He's staying here with his wife."

"Fascinating," I say, finally locating the corkscrew.

"Would you be so kind as to flip this coin?" He's holding out a fifty-pence piece. "Heads, I reveal to the local paper that he's fudged his taxes. Tails, I sleep with his wife."

"Right," I say. Surely he's not actually serious. The cork comes free from the bottle with a squeaky pop. He's still holding out the coin.

"Fine!" I say and take it from him. I throw it onto the bar. "Heads," I tell him. "Poor old Mrs. Grassingham."

"Not to worry." Jamie grins. "I'll probably pay her a visit anyway. She assured me her room would be unlocked—and 'old Mrs. Grassingham' is a bit unfair. She's only twenty-seven."

Chapter 8

When I arrive the next day for my late shift, there is no sign of Melanie, who's supposed to be on the bar with Suzy.

"No way, look!" says Dan, pointing into the conservatory.

Melanie is out on the back terrace, talking to Jamie. He gestures for her to follow him, and she looks around. Her face is pink and flustered. They disappear along the path that leads to the pool house.

"Oh my God!" says Suzy.

Dan shakes his head. "No way," he says again.

I have a sudden urge to follow them. But what am I going to do—watch?

"Do you want a hand at the bar?" Dan asks Suzy.

"No, I should be fine," she replies. "There's only one old guy there ordering whiskey, and he hasn't moved for a while. I might go and make sure he's not dead."

When she's gone, Dan turns to me. "Hello," he says with a grin.

"Hello," I reply, and we start chatting about the shift he's just finished. Before I know it, twenty minutes have gone by and I have to go get changed.

I find the servants' quarters, where there are lockers, showers, and a changing room the staff can use. As I get near the shower room, I can hear water running. I have a wild thought that it's Jamie and Melanie and that they came in here instead of going to the pool house. They'll probably have locked the door if it is. I try the doorknob and it opens. My mind is running through things I might see and how I probably shouldn't want to see them. I'm just curious; it's so unbelievable.

I walk in, and at first I can't see anything through the steam. Then the running water turns off and the shower door swings open.

It's not Jamie.

It's a girl.

And she's completely naked.

Chapter 9

The girl looks at me with mild surprise but doesn't seem too bothered that I've just walked in on her. Which is in complete contrast to me, standing frozen in awkwardness.

"Hello!" I say in a way that reminds me of Jeff. Or someone else old.

She has an angular face with sharp features, skin that is a coffee color, and long, dark hair cascading in dripping strands around her head. And no clothes, obviously. Her long, slim legs glisten, and she has small, round breasts that I am finding it hard not to stare at. It's not that easy to keep eye contact with someone who's naked. But when I do concentrate on her face, I think I know her, and then I realize—she's the girl from Jamie's Facebook pictures. This is Cleo.

"I'm s—" I start to say and then inhale a ton of steam and start coughing.

44

She looks at me coolly. "Got a towel?"

"Um, yeah, in here somewhere." I fumble with my bag. With a pang of embarrassment, I realize I've brought Matthew's old Thomas the Tank Engine towel. "It's my little brother's," I mumble.

She shrugs and takes it. "I forgot mine." She pats her body dry and then starts drying her hair, not covering up anything at all. "You're new," she says.

"I'm Mia. I started last week."

"He said there was a new one. He'll like you. Petite. Brunette. Good boobs."

"Oh"—I have literally no idea what to say—"thank you."

She's blocking me from getting to the bench but doesn't seem to have noticed.

"Um, Cleo, could I—"

She's in the middle of tying the towel around herself and looks up at me through her hair. "Stalker..."

I freeze. Crap. I am a stalker. I literally stalked her on Facebook and have just announced it by knowing her name.

"Joke," she says. "You've heard of me. That's great."

She says everything in a low, lazy way, like life bores her. I put my bag down on the bench and start getting changed. Another high-waisted black skirt and fitted white shirt. But I've got more makeup on today. Usually I just throw on a bit of mascara and lip gloss a few minutes before I leave the house, but today Gabi has gone all out by giving me smoky eyes as part of the Dan plan. I wonder if Jamie notices stuff like that. Cleo doesn't have a makeup bag with her or anything, just a pile of clothes that she doesn't appear to be changing into. She's sitting on the bench in my towel watching me get changed.

"When do you finish?"

"At eleven. But we have to clean up after that."

"I'll come by the bar. We'll have a drink."

"I can't really—my stepdad's picking me up."

I'm in my clothes now and starting to leave. Cleo gets up and moves between me and the door. Still wearing my towel. I hope I haven't accidentally given it to her forever. She opens the door for me to leave but is still in my way.

"Call him and cancel. It'll be fun. We'll get shit-faced, and end up fucking some waiters."

"That's rather sordid, dear." Jamie has appeared at the door.

"Piss off, Jay," Cleo retorts, moving back into the room a little.

"I'm sure this delightful little waitress doesn't want to be dragged into your debauched world."

"No," I say, "but she would like to go serve tiny food to your guests, so if you could let her through, that would be great."

"Well, if you think so little of the food, then don't feel you have to hang around and serve it," Jamie says, not moving out of my way. "There are plenty more where you came from."

I suddenly panic. What if he pours port down my shirt and gets me fired?

It must show on my face, because he laughs.

"Take a joke, Joseph. But we should be getting along." He still doesn't move. "Melanie's fascinating fiancé, Simon, has arrived to pick her up, and I've got some lovely photos to show him."

46

Clearly I'm going to have to just barge my way out. For a second I am sandwiched between them. Cleo says, "Drinks later? I won't take no for an answer."

I sigh. I'm going to be late if I don't get out of here. "Fine."

"Fabulous," purrs Cleo.

Jamie eyes me as I push past him. "Have a *fabulous* time, Joseph."

When I get to the restaurant, I start laying out cutlery. I keep losing concentration and having to check that I've put the right things in the right order. Jamie's naked girlfriend and the way he was looking at her keep popping into my head. She's so confident. I doubt there are many girls who would tell Jamie to piss off. Maybe that's why she's his girlfriend.

I drop a spoon and bend down to pick it up. You don't see naked people very often. Maybe in some magazines or online, but Cleo is my age. The only people my age I've seen naked are Gabi and Kieran. Gabi thinks it's funny when you stay over at her house to wake you up by flashing or mooning you.

I'm going to have to stop thinking about this, or when the first guests come in I might accidentally say "boobs" to them instead of "menu" or "Can I take your order?"

Suddenly there's a shriek from the front of the castle. All of the staff head over to see what's going on.

It's Melanie and a tall guy with a big nose, who I instantly recognize as Simon because I've seen about a million pictures of him on Melanie's phone having a Turkish mud bath. They're having a blazing fight in the front parking lot.

"What the HELL, Mel?" he yells, and covers his eyes.

She grabs on to his jacket and tries to get herself into his line of sight.

"No! No, he said it would be a nice thing—some nice photos of...of..."

"Of you in your underwear?" Simon is looking at her now, but not in the way she wants, I'd imagine—more like he's wondering whether she's gone insane.

"He said it was for *us*!" she pleads. "I was going to show you! Like a prewedding gift! I didn't know he would send...He must have taken my phone." Her eyes dart upward.

At the top of the main entrance door, one floor up, there is an enclosed stone balcony. Jamie's leaning casually on the ledge. He gives Melanie a wave and a grin and holds up a phone. *Her* phone. He presses a few buttons, and there's a short delay before Simon's phone beeps. He looks at the message.

"Jesus Christ, not another one!" He looks at it. "Topless?"

Mel is sobbing now. "He...He said it was arty," she says miserably.

Jamie then tosses the phone from the balcony and Melanie puts her hands out to catch it. She misses and it lands on the gravel. The screen is completely smashed. She scrambles to pick it up and then turns it over and gives a little cry. The case—a "pacifically designed" one, as she put it, featuring a picture of her and Simon and inscribed *M & S 4eva* in gold—has a long crack through it.

"Okay," Simon says, gearing himself up. "Okay. I'm going to talk to him." He strides purposefully along the gravel and through the reception door.

Melanie whimpers weakly. No one else can think of anything to say.

A minute later he strides purposefully out again.

"Where are the stairs?"

Chapter 10

"Oh man! That was crazy. Pretty funny, though," says Andreas as we head back to the restaurant.

I don't say anything. It's not funny at all to me, and I'm feeling that familiar wave of cold panic. The thing I felt for weeks after Kieran. I think it's finally gone, and then something reminds me. I look quickly at Dan to see if he's noticed my reaction. He looks concerned. *Please don't let him know,* I pray silently.

"Hilaire!" says a girl's voice followed by giggling, and I realize that two girls who aren't waitresses are here as well. They have their hair piled on top of their heads, and one has a real Prada bag slung over her shoulder, so they must be guests. My mom has one of those, and it's her prize possession. She won't even let me borrow it because she says I'll stretch it. I'm not exactly sure how she thinks I would do that. These two girls look only about fourteen, though.

They seem like they're searching for someone and disappear through to the courtyard while we head to the restaurant.

When I go out onto the terrace to clear some tables, they appear again, walking through the arches, clearly having tracked down the person they were looking for.

They break into a bouncing run toward another girl sitting with her knees drawn up to her chest on the low stone wall that goes around the terrace. She's tiny and delicate, probably what people would call waiflike, with long, wavy blond hair under a huge floppy white hat, which makes her look even smaller. She has huge sunglasses on too, so only a tiny bit of her face is actually visible. The other two spring up to her in a flurry of excitement.

"Omigod, Jay's so hilaire! You'll *nahver* guess, Dez."

She frowns at them and says, in a sweet, tinkling voice, "My brother's a dick." Then her head snaps to the side and she looks straight at me. I realize that I've stopped next to the table I'm clearing and I am just watching them. She tilts her head forward so that the sunglasses fall onto her nose. "What?"

I hurriedly start clearing the glasses. She's got the same deep brown eyes as Jamie; they bore into you like lasers.

On my way back to the kitchen, I plan to tell Dan that I've finally seen the other child that Julia goes on about, but as I near the door, I hear Dan talking to someone, and I've got a pretty good idea who it is.

"Come on, man, you broke the girl's phone. We don't get paid that much, you know."

"Oh, don't tell me the peasants are revolting." I move closer to see Jamie's helping himself to strawberries from the dessert cart. "Fine, I'll buy her a new one. Or she could sell the pictures if she wants an upgrade."

51

He moves to leave, but Dan is in his way, holding the dishwasher tray full of glasses.

"Excuse me, pot washer."

Dan doesn't say anything.

"Mr. Pot Washer?"

"I've got a name, actually."

"Oh, do you? Don't tell me, Sparky or something? Smudger? The plucky kid from the streets?"

Dan laughs and shakes his head. "Whatever, man."

He lets Jamie past, and Jamie sees me hovering at the door. "I'll look forward to the pleasure of your company later, Joseph," he says and holds the door open for me.

"You won't," I say quickly, even though it doesn't make sense. Dan looks sharply in our direction.

"We'll see. Don't bring your thug."

I put my tray down and start loading the glasses into the dishwasher tray.

"I've got those," Dan says in a clipped voice.

"I'm meeting Cleo for a drink after work." I feel I have to explain. "She's his girlfriend." I'm trying to sound casual, but it comes out exaggeratedly cheerful.

"Oh, cool. Sounds fun," he says, and then rams the tray of glasses into the dishwasher a bit more forcefully than usual.

"I probably won't even go," I say.

Dan shrugs. "Going to get my bag."

He comes back a few minutes later in a rugby shirt with the sleeves rolled up. He leans against the door and looks serious.

"Did I tell you I lost my left side?" he says gravely.

"What?"

"Yeah, I'm all right now."

He grins and I groan, but it turns into a laugh. I get a rush of warmth and want him to stay and hang out with me while I work my shift. He cocks his head to the side. "You in tomorrow?"

"Yep," I say, the tension from a few minutes ago falling away. "Got my first early shift."

"I'm on early too. Want to do something after?"

I get a warm buzz in my chest, just like the first time Kieran texted me. Except this time I don't feel the need to think up a cool response.

"Yeah, definitely."

I can't stop smiling to myself after he's gone. I bounce around the kitchen in a good mood and even offer to help Omar, the chef, make the salads. He says, "No, lady," and moves the bowl of tomatoes away from me, but I just give him a grin and head merrily out to the bar. I check to make sure no guests, or Julia, are around, then take my phone out and text Gabi.

Dan plan update—"doing something" after work tomorrow! X

Her reply is almost instantaneous.

YES! OMG!! When n where? Gonna come stalk you. JOKE. But seriously wen can I come get free food? x

The shift is pretty quiet. Hardly any tables come in, and Suzy's time is mostly taken up by the old guy steadily ordering more whiskey and giving her more tips. Ben, who's on in the kitchen, goes home early, and soon it's just me left.

I lean back against the dishwasher, willing the clock to reach eleven. Feeling the cool steel on my back, I immediately think of Gabi's dishwasher comment about me and Dan. I get that warm buzzy feeling again, remembering him leaning on the door frame, his rolled-up rugby shirtsleeves showing off the curves of his muscles. It's like whenever he's near me, I just want to hug him. What if it happens, one night at the end of a shift, and he just walks up and kisses me?

I put my head back against the dishwasher, imagining it's his kiss moving me. I think of his hands running over me, in my hair and down my back. Like on my interview day when Jamie was kissing that waitress in the window and she would have felt the weight of his body pressed against her.

Dan's kiss would be soft and smooth, I decide, and he'd start kissing my neck. I feel stubble grazing my skin. Suddenly, the brown hair I'm running my fingers through turns blond, and the chest pushed up against me is wearing an expensive shirt. He pulls his head back and fixes me with those dark eyes. For a second we stare at each other, and then he kisses the base of my neck, and lower, and lower, and his hands are on my legs, pushing up my skirt.

Chapter 11

There's a loud clang as my arm goes back, knocking a saucepan off the counter, and I cry out. The kitchen door swings open and I panic that it's Jamie, that he was watching me and he knows what I was thinking. Did I say anything out loud? He's even creeping up on me in my own head.

"Drink time!" It's Cleo. "What's your name again?"

"Mia," I say, willing my heart to stop thumping in my chest and my breathing to return to normal. My face is burning. I must look crazy.

"Do you want some clothes?" says Cleo.

She's looking at my skirt and I smooth it down, trying to banish images of Jamie's hands from my brain. "I've got what I came here in."

"Sorry, I mean do you want some less shitty clothes?"

I briefly consider taking the rudeness and letting Cleo dress me up in expensive clothes, but to be honest, I'm a little pissed off at people ordering me around when I'm not even working.

"Um, no, thanks. I'm all right." There's a miniature Gabi in my head facepalming herself. Gabi has significant debt due to an obsession with expensive clothes.

Cleo spins on her heel and heads to the bar, and I tell her I'm going to put on my (shitty) clothes. Back in the changing room and in my skater dress, I text Jeff to tell him I'm staying later and ask if he can get me at twelve thirty. I get a grumpy reply yes. There's a text on there from Dan too, suggesting a picnic for tomorrow.

A picnic. Dan's so thoughtful and nice and normal. He wouldn't have sex with politicians' wives or take pictures of girls and send them to their boyfriends. I forward the text to Gabi because we made this rule when we were younger that we would share important boy-related texts, and we still do it when there's a new boy on the scene. Once she was officially with Max, I told her she could stop sharing hers. Mostly because they were gross.

I realize there's a text lurking on my phone that I haven't shared.

Gabi replies to my Dan text with a smiley face.

I suddenly wonder why I'm even going for this drink with a girl I hardly know. I didn't have to say yes. Am I thinking that Cleo and Jamie will take me to hang out with their elite gang? It would be the first time in a while I've hung out in a group. I've been avoiding social occasions recently. Even though all the girls totally froze out Kieran, we were still friends with guys from his school, and there was always the chance of bumping into him, and I couldn't face that.

I missed all the end-of-finals stuff and even the Year

Eleven prom; I had a dress and everything. Mom took me out shopping to cheer me up because I'd broken up with Kieran. She thought I was just sad because I loved him so much. She didn't know I was constantly panicking that people were talking about me. But the shopping trip really worked for a while. We tried on stupid clothes and Mom got stuck in some skinny jeans and I couldn't even help her because I was laughing so much watching her struggle. But then I saw some of Kieran's friends in town and I was sure they were looking at me and whispering to each other.

I sat in my room on the day of the prom in my pajamas just looking at my dress hanging there. My phone kept buzzing with texts from Gabi, starting with, `You ready babe? X` and ending with, `ARE YOU DEAD?` before I finally replied `I'm sorry, I'm not going x`.

Gabi offered to come over, which was really lovely of her, but I wasn't having any of it, as she'd been going on about the prom all year and getting to see Max in black tie (he still wore his hat, apparently). But just the idea of everyone being there freaked me out, even though I felt miserable sitting like a loner in my room when I knew everyone was on their way to the prom in a limo. Mom didn't say anything about the dress. She put her pajamas on too, banished Jeff and Matthew from the front room, and we watched *The Notebook* and ate pizza.

I walk back along the dark, echoey corridor toward the bar, thinking that I'll tell Cleo I'm actually feeling pretty wiped out and will just get picked up now.

But when I see her sitting up on a bar stool, she's already poured me a glass of champagne.

"Oh, actually you look all right," she says, holding out a glass.

"Um, thanks." I clamber onto the bar stool in front of her, wishing I could develop a way of gliding elegantly around at all times. Or just having longer legs. Or a different body and personality.

"We'll head over to the pool house later if you like. Jay's got some of his sad little friends there. It's pretty fun watching them basically kiss his ass."

She clinks her glass on mine. "So who *are* you, Mia?" She's looking right at me now. Like she really wants to know about my dull life.

I start tentatively, saying "um" a lot, and tell her where I live and go to school. Is it possible to bore someone to death? I feel like I'm making a very good attempt.

But Cleo seems interested. She pushes her hair back from her face, emphasizing her flawless skin, and smiles warmly at me while she tops up my glass. Her accent has a hint of something that I can't place. I bet she's traveled to all sorts of exotic places and has stories a hundred times more interesting than me informing her that I have a cat and a brother. I tell her about my traveling plan and how I'm going to try to get around my mom. I realize that I'm talking a lot.

"What about you?" I ask, trying to even things up.

"What about me? Dad's a sultan; Mom's a whore. Lived all over, but they've dumped me here for now." She pauses as she finishes her glass. "A bit of stability so I don't fuck up my exams and miss out on Oxbridge." She pours another, and I notice there's a second bottle waiting in an ice bucket behind her. I'm about to take a sip but put my glass back down. After two glasses I'm already feeling the effects, and if I carry on at this speed I'm going to be trashed.

"So, how did you meet—"

58

"Jamie? Some charity gala thing. While this fat old biddy was making a speech about wonderful Jamie raising lots of money for them by climbing a mountain or some shit, he appeared behind me, whispering how he wanted to do unspeakable things to me."

"Did he?" I say, not really sure what I'm asking.

"Some of them." She shrugs. "Most of them, actually. But never all the way."

"Really? You haven't?"

She shakes her head. "He won't admit he loves me. That's my demand. He can't say it. He says he doesn't care, that he's not some slobbering teen desperate to get laid. But I know it drives him crazy when there's something he can't have. He's had it easy all his life, and then I come along and I'm difficult."

"Do you want it to be difficult, though? I mean, shouldn't a relationship be easy? Just hanging out and making each other laugh and stuff?"

"And getting married, and having kids, and losing ten years while you're covered in baby puke and putting on weight till you sit at brunch talking about little Oscar's stupid entrance exam because that's all you've got in your awful boring life? Difficult is fun. It means there's passion. You almost hate them, but you've never wanted anything more."

I shift in my chair, and it feels like the champagne bubbles are going up and down my legs. She fills up my glass, then fixes me with her wide brown eyes. "One thing. Just don't kiss him."

I give a nervous half laugh. "Um, okay...I didn't—"

"He's got this thing," she says. "He can make you come just by kissing you."

I shift again and cross my legs. It's not the champagne this time.

"So," says Cleo, leaning back again, the intense moment past, "what about you?"

I look down at my glass. "Nothing very exciting. There was this one guy—my ex."

I trail off, a hot, tense feeling gathering in my chest. I swallow.

Cleo leans closer with her chin on her hand. "Yeah?" she says softly.

There's a lump in my throat, but I push the words out. "He was kind of a dick when we broke up."

She puts her hand on mine and smiles sympathetically. Her skin feels impossibly smooth, and her nails are perfectly manicured. "Let it out," she says. "You'll feel better."

I look at her. I find it really hard to say any of this stuff. Even Gabi has to coax it out of me. But for some reason, maybe because Cleo's a stranger and doesn't know Kieran, I feel the words forming, ready to leave my mouth.

I start talking. I tell her everything. The stuff that only Gabi knows. While I do, the champagne flows. There's something else as well: I have this weird urge to impress Cleo and be taken into her confidence. She has this intense way of looking at you, of making you feel like you're the only person she's interested in. Even though I know she probably does it to everyone, it still works. I know she's running the show, confidently drawing out words and feelings I haven't spoken about in forever, and casually revealing intimate details about herself to make it seem like a conversation. And every time she does, I get this thrill.

"So, that guy. Not good. But what do you think about when you masturbate?"

I choke on nothing, which she probably doesn't find particularly normal. It makes my eyes water.

"Don't tell me you haven't. How do you know what you like if you've never done it to yourself, or imagined it?"

"No, I mean, yeah, I have, but..." I swallow and try to will my face not to turn bright red.

She fixes me with a knowing look. "Do it more. And better. Spend time on it. Use things. Not just a thirty-second fumble and you're done."

This is possibly the weirdest pep talk I've ever had. But the excitement of talking about something I never talk about, despite Gabi's best efforts, is burning in my chest. "O-okay." I laugh, holding up my empty glass. "I promise."

She laughs. "Good."

I try to focus on the clock on the wall. It's a quarter past midnight. "I'm getting picked up soon." I look back at Cleo and the room lurches.

She shakes her head. "No, I don't think so." She grabs my phone out of my bag. "What's your stepdad's name—Johnny?"

"Jeff. Wait, what are you doing?"

"*Jeff...am...staying...over...,*" she says as she types.

"No!" I try to snatch the phone back.

She wriggles out of my way and bats at my hand. I sway on the stool, and the room spins a bit. I reach my hand out to steady myself and accidentally put it in the ice bucket. "*No need for lift...*"

I go for the phone again, but she puts her hand on my face and pushes me back, finishing the text with the other hand. "*Thanks!* And, send."

"He's going to be so pissed off," I say, but I can't help

61

laughing. Sure enough, the reply comes through. He's been waiting up; this is inconsiderate, etc. The letters are going a little blurry. Cleo bites her lip in mock worry. "Sorry."

I get a wave of confidence (or it could be nausea) and toss the phone aside. "Whatever. He should know that lots of other people—even other teachers—don't go to bed at nine on a Saturday."

Cleo laughs, encouraging me to keep going with the random crap that's falling out of my mouth.

"He's a geek and a loser."

Cleo grabs my hand. "Come on. Into the devil's lair."

Chapter 12

I can see flickering lights up ahead as I stumble toward the pool house. Cleo's dragging me forward forcefully, which is fortunate, really, because otherwise I would probably veer off into the pool and drown.

As we get closer, it looks like the pool house is glowing. Between the pillars are three floor-to-ceiling doors, all wide open and flinging light onto the water. Inside is an open-plan kitchen and living room with a stone floor, white walls, and arching wooden beams forming the roof. I spot two doors along the back walls that are closed but must lead to the bedroom and bathroom. There are people sitting in groups everywhere, and Jamie holds court from a mahogany armchair surrounded by girls. He watches us, but Cleo leads me to the other side of the room where two girls are sitting.

"This is Nish and Effy," Cleo says. "They're lesbians."

"Oh, good," I say and mentally kick my brain.

"They're my only female friends. Every other girl in here is trying to sleep with my boyfriend."

I try to look at Nish and Effy, but really all I see are outlines of hair and a glittery headband.

From then on everything happens in flashes, a series of images and clips of conversation. For a while I am on a sofa talking to a guy with a mop of wavy red hair. I'm saying, "You're William?"

"I'm Willem," he assures me.

"William," I tell him.

"Will-em."

I shake my lopsided head at him. "No, no. That's not a real name."

He melts away and then I'm by the side of the drinks table and a guy with spiky black hair leans over to whisper something in my ear and at the same time puts his hand on my butt.

Cleo appears and rescues me. "Hands off, cretin."

I blink and suddenly I am sitting on the steps outside. I'm with a guy who possibly just told me he's named Toby and has a friendly smile and lots of curly hair. He's smoking a joint and I ask for some, telling him, for some unknown reason, that I do it all the time. Just a tiny bit has my head swimming and fiery tingles racing through my hands and feet. The next thing I know, I'm poking the boy and showing him my hand. "Toby, Toby, my finger's on fire!"

A hand grabs the back of my dress and pulls me up. Perhaps it's Jamie. Perhaps he'll kiss me.

It's Cleo. "Come on. We're dancing."

My eyes struggle to adjust to the darkness after sitting by the lights around the pool. Drum and bass music reverberate through the floor, and bodies all around me are moving in a blur. There's Cleo's face at the center, and we start moving. For the first time in a long time, I'm doing crazy dancing and I don't care. And then Cleo's hands are on my face. She pulls me forward and our lips meet. I can taste the alcohol on her mouth, which spreads through my body, and I kiss her back.

"A little attention-seeking, even for you." His voice comes from behind me.

Cleo pulls back and smiles at him, triumphant. She drops her hands back down to her sides and I stumble backward, into his hard chest.

"Oh, dear. What would the pot washer say?" His jaw is level with the top of my head. I slow my breathing down. I need water.

"Okay!" he shouts, almost giving me a heart attack. "Turn off this drivel." And he's gone from behind me. A moment later the music cuts out and there's the scratch of a record starting. It's something classical and dramatic.

As the conversation dies and people gradually start to look at Jamie, I use the pause to go to the sink and get water. Jamie looks over at me, and I feel good that I'm not immediately jumping to attention. I try to saunter back over like I don't really care what he's going to do, but I keep a hand on the kitchen counter to maintain my balance, because I think the sauntering will probably lose its effect if I fall on my face.

Jamie sits back in his chair. "You look like you've just learned to walk."

I try to think of something funny and biting to say, but my brain is mostly full of swirling, so I just roll my eyes.

Cleo sits on the arm of Jamie's chair, and the girl who was previously on the other arm scuttles away. I sink down to sit on what I realize too late is not a chair, but a footstool.

"Please, God, let's do something interesting," he says to the room in general. "What do you have for me? Who's played the game?"

A girl with frizzy hair and unfortunately large teeth springs to her feet. "I've got something!"

"Ah, Christina. I asked you to do something for me, didn't I? What did I ask you to do?"

"To...to mess with Lady Michaels."

"Now, Joseph," says Jamie, leaning over close enough for me to feel his breath, "we don't like Lady Michaels. Lady Michaels was awfully rude to my mother." I feel all the eyes in the room swivel in my direction.

"I, uh, got, um, chatting to Lord Michaels," Christina says and snorts.

"Lord Michaels. Excellent choice. He's a sucker for a young girl's face. Even yours, Christina."

"I know!" Christina nods her head, eyes wide, missing the insult. "He sent me pictures of his thingy!"

She hands her phone to Jamie, who looks at it and winces. "That's a lot to put up with for a title. Connors?"

"Yup." A small guy with a pale, pinched face stands up and then seems to shrink on realizing he has the attention of the room. My vision is less blurry now, but I've got a cloud of pain churning in my head.

"Could you see to it that these pictures are uploaded to the homepage of Platinum PR? A slideshow would be nice, with captions to explain that these are images sent by the CEO's husband to a seventeen-year-old."

Howls of appreciation go up from the room. Connors takes the phone and busies himself in a corner at an iMac.

"Another marriage wrecked. Well done, Jay," says Cleo sweetly.

"A cold, vacuous one," Jamie says. "It's her career that matters to her."

The words are flowing past me and I can't process them.

"You guys are weird," I eventually manage.

Jamie looks at me, and for a second I think he's moving his head from side to side, which would be an odd thing for him to do. Then I realize it's my drunk brain.

Meanwhile, a rowdy conversation has broken out. Apparently the redhead, Willem, has an attractive mother, and everyone is one-upping each other with what they'd do to her. The boy with the black spiky hair is acting it out, graphically. Willem's cheeks turn pink and he snaps, "I bet that's what you do to your own mom."

The black-haired guy leans in close to him. "I'm not pussy enough to let people talk about my mom that way."

Jamie stands up. "No, Guy, no one talks about your mom that way, because she's fat and unattractive. Now, could you all go home? I want to go to bed."

I steady myself on the footstool. Now to try to get myself to the servants' quarters, ideally without waking up any guests and definitely without waking up Julia. As the crowd leaves, Guy is muttering something, and I catch the word "sister." Jamie does too, and he watches him leave. I see a flicker of something in his eyes that is sharp and not like his usual bored expression.

"You can stay here," he says to me.

I start to protest, but he interrupts by throwing me a blanket.

"Keep your pants on. I meant on the sofa."

"What if I don't want to?"

"Then, by all means, take your pants off."

"Give her some pajamas, Jay," says Cleo, emerging from the bedroom wearing a white negligee that comes down only to the top of her thighs.

Jamie tosses me a bundle of clothes, which I unravel into a T-shirt and some boxers. I go to the bathroom and get changed. Looking at myself in the mirror, I get a vision of me standing next to Cleo. Her light brown skin sets off the startling white of the silk resting on it. She almost shimmers. I have very attractive gray skin and a slightly cross-eyed look from the alcohol. At least, I hope it's the alcohol and I don't usually look like I recently died.

I lie down on the velvet sofa, and wrap myself in the blanket with my head on a ridiculously soft cushion. The room is still spinning slightly, and I know I'm going to feel awful tomorrow.

I force myself to get up again. If I don't have another glass or two of water, there's no way I will be able to work. The stone slab floor is freezing on my bare feet. When I get to the sink, my eye catches some movement to my left.

Jamie's bedroom door is open, and I can see the top half of his bed. He's lying back, wearing just his boxers, and reading a book. He has his knees bent and one hand behind his head. His chest rises and falls, and my eyes are pulled toward his toned stomach, following a line of hair that leads down to the top of his boxers.

He's got a small frown of concentration. I want to call over and ask what he's reading, but then I see Cleo. She comes crawling up between his legs and grips the wrist of the hand holding the book. She pushes his arm back so that both his hands are above his head, and the book falls to the floor. She puts her face close to his, about to kiss him, but then moves down again, her lips brushing over his neck, chest, and stomach and stopping at the top of his boxers. Then she comes up again, doing the same thing, and Jamie's back arches.

Flustered, I turn the tap with more force than I mean to, and a jet of water comes gushing out. I keep looking forward at the glass, so that if they do look over, it doesn't seem like I was watching them.

I hear the door close.

Chapter 13

I'm on the sofa, lying on my front. Wait, no... This is one of the lounge chairs by the pool. I'm wearing a bikini and I'm waiting there for him. Sure enough, I sense someone behind me, and then hands grip mine. But the hands are coffee colored, with perfectly manicured nails. I feel long hair brushing my shoulders. I struggle to get free and feel lips brushing up and down my back. I twist around and look up. Cleo grins at me.

"Come on. We've got to get to the devil's lair."

We run hand in hand along the side of the pool and onto a path I've never seen before. Suddenly it transforms into a dusty red path that starts going upward and around in circles. We're running up a mountain. When we reach the top, I can see for miles around. The sky is shot through with pink; the sun is beginning to rise. She takes my other hand and I realize that it's not Cleo—it's Jamie. He leans forward and kisses me gently on the forehead. He rests his head against mine and looks down at me. "I love you."

As my eyes flicker open, there's a blurry face above me. The same one that just said he loved me.

"'Morning."

I draw the covers up to my chin. "Were you watching me sleep?" I say, mostly out of panic that I said something weird. But then, watching me sleep would be pretty creepy too.

"Don't flatter yourself." He plonks a plate on the coffee table next to the sofa. "You'll need this."

It's a bacon-and-egg sandwich. I raise my head with a groan. There's classical music playing again, and the violins feel like someone sawing at my skull. He turns it down.

"I was drowning out your snoring."

He sits down next to me on the sofa, giving me no choice but to sit up. He's got a black T-shirt and boxers on, and when he sits down, our bare legs are touching.

"Where's Cleo?"

"On a walk? She likes to keep me in the dark."

He puts his foot on his knee and rests his book on his leg. It means his leg is now digging into me. I hadn't noticed he wears glasses for reading.

"It's really off-putting, having you stare at me," he says, without turning to look at me.

"What are you reading?"

He tilts the front cover toward me about an inch.

"I can't read it."

"That's a little worrying, at your age."

"I mean, I can't see it."

"*Ancient Greek Myths and Legends.*"

"Oh! Right."

"What were you expecting?" He still doesn't look up from the book, but I don't think he's reading it anymore, as his eyes aren't moving. He's waiting for my reply.

"Something intellectual and douche-y." Apparently constantly repressing the urge to be sick means I don't care what I say to him.

I see a smile at the corners of his mouth, but he turns the page pointedly and doesn't say anything.

I pick up the sandwich and take a tiny, feeble bite. "Did you make this?"

"No, I got your kitchen friend to do it. Smudger."

"What—Dan? He's there already? Am I late for work? What time is it?"

He throws his head back on the sofa. "Don't give yourself a seizure. Yes, 'Dan.' Yes, he's there already. No, you're not late. I have no idea why Mr. Pot Washer is here. It's only a quarter to seven. In the morning."

I stand up, and Jamie grabs the back of my T-shirt and I fall back against the sofa. He has his head to the side, looking at me.

"I'd like my clothes back."

"Well, I wasn't going to wear them to work."

"You'd better take them off, then."

"I will. In your bathroom."

He's doing his curious, amused look at me again. I feel the urge to move along the sofa toward him. I look at his lips. They're just a few inches away. Our legs are still touching.

Jamie looks like he's about to say something. I get that nervous feeling again. If Cleo came back in here now, this might look…odd.

"Okay, I'm going." I stand up quickly. Too quickly. I get

a massive head rush and fall forward onto the coffee table and end up with my ass in the air.

Jamie laughs. "I didn't know you were in heat."

"Oh, shut up," I grumble as I scramble to my feet and then stomp off to the bathroom.

"No, really. It's an interesting seduction technique," he calls after me.

"Don't flatter yourself," I say, hopefully with "attitude." Then I ruin it by walking into the door frame. I try to tell myself he didn't see, but he definitely did.

"Joseph?" Jamie says when I emerge a few minutes later after the quickest shower and clothes-change known to man. I've just gotten to the door, and I turn back.

"You have a lovely smile," he says.

I smile at him involuntarily.

There's a mist hanging over the castle as I walk back along the stony path away from the pool house. It makes the two back turrets look magical. I wonder if Jamie is watching me go.

Then I see Cleo coming through the arches, going the other way. She waves and flashes me a warm smile. I wave back and say, "Hey!" but there's an uneasiness clinging to my voice. I don't want her to think I'm just another girl hanging around the pool house trying to sleep with her boyfriend. Because I'm not.

Chapter 14

Work today is every kind of hell. Any part of my body that can ache is doing exactly that. Jamie and Cleo loll lazily at one of the tables outside. I try to avoid them and let Andreas serve them as much as possible. But now Omar hands me a cheeseboard and says, "Table sixteen." I ask if Andreas can do it, but Omar says, "You take. Lazy." So I do.

There's a breeze coming from across the grounds that blows my hair across my face. At least I can hide behind it. Cleo's wearing massive sunglasses, so I think she's suffering too. I plonk the plate down and Cleo says, "Feeling good this morning?"

"My blood hurts," I say shortly and stomp back to the kitchen. Jamie's laughter follows me in.

My suffering is turning into a running joke among the other waiters. They keep trying to get me to take out the garbage and other jobs that will definitely make me puke.

Dan hasn't spoken to me yet. He's hanging out by the bar, and I haven't gone over. I wonder if he'll be funny about me going to the party. I get the feeling it's a bit "us" and "them" between the staff and Jamie and his friends. Not surprising, since we're working and they're lounging around doing nothing. I should be more loyal to "us."

As I go back and forth around the tables, I glance over at Dan as he polishes glasses and chats to Suzy. I get a pang of jealousy when I hear them laughing together. It's stupid, but I wish his silly jokes were just for me.

I still haven't spoken to him by the time it's three o'clock and our shifts end. I get a feeling of definite grimness when I remember I have to now change back into the dress I was wearing last night. It's not how I was planning to impress him on our picnic that might be kind of a date.

I wait for him outside reception, but after ten minutes, there's no sign of him. Maybe he's gone home and the date's off. He's heard about my antics last night and thinks I'm not the sort of girl he'd take on a picnic. To be honest, as well as mortifying, the thought is a tiny bit relieving. I still feel so bad that I just want to go home and curl up in bed while my mom brings me a cup of tea.

Dan emerges from the reception door. He's brought a picnic basket. He's in his jeans and another rugby shirt and he's shielding his eyes from the sun.

"Come on," he says, smiling at me. "I've found this really great place."

We walk through the grounds away from the castle, but instead of going alongside the river, Dan veers off the path and up into a forest. It's a nature preserve, apparently. I never even knew it was here. The ground angles steeply upward, and we push our way through long grass and ferns. The canopy of trees plunges us into shadow, with occasional sunlight glinting through the branches. I breathe in; it smells fresh, and it seems as though my head instantly clears. Now that the trees are enclosing us from all sides, I can imagine that we're trekking somewhere—somewhere foreign, exciting, and not here.

I should do it, I think. Keep saving and then just go. I could even go with Dan.

No, that's probably a stupid idea. I hardly know him.

But by the end of the summer I would.

Dan's a few yards ahead and calls out, "Here we are!"

There's a break in the trees, and as I walk out I'm dazzled for a moment by the sunlight bursting through. We're at the top of a hill, looking out over a lake and, in the distance, more hills and fields. It's beautiful.

Dan lays down a blanket. "I don't know about you, but I'm starving." I kneel down and he opens the hamper. "Now, I psychically worked out your favorite food. That's right—I know what you love most is leftovers from work!"

I laugh. "So you saw me lurking around the garbage cans, picking up scraps, then?"

"Oh, yes." He's unwrapping little packets of foil now. There are honey-glazed sausages, salmon mousse canapés, and slices of olive bread. "And," he says with a flourish, "fizzy grape juice, because I think there's a good chance you don't want wine right now."

There's a lump rising in my throat, and for a moment I feel like crying. This is all so nice. I blink a few times to try to stop tears from coming into my eyes.

Dan looks a bit taken aback, understandably. Most people

76

don't cry when offered a sausage. "You look like you could use a hug."

His expression is kind and smiley, with no hidden meanings. I feel my heart melt with gratitude.

"Well, my mom gives the best hugs, but I suppose you'll do."

"I can pretend. I'm told I look good in an apron."

He wraps his arms around me and I press my head against his chest. It's warm and comforting and exactly what I want. I blow out a long breath, and it feels like the first time I've breathed this morning. I move my head back to look at him.

"Thanks for that."

His face is serious. "Well, it was pretty horrible for me…"

We both laugh, and then suddenly I lean forward and kiss him lightly on the lips.

"Thanks for that," he says, half smiling.

I sit back down on the grass, surprised at myself. I'm never the first to go for the kiss. Usually my head's full of paranoid thoughts like, *What if he's so repulsed by my kissing him he throws up?* or *What if I kiss wrong and no one ever told me?* or *What if he wants to go further and I'm not sure?* But right here, in this place with Dan, it doesn't feel like part of normal life.

"So, last night. Did you kiss all the boys?" Dan holds out a bowl full of strawberries.

"Ha. Yep, every last one."

My stomach lurches as a memory comes back to me. Oh my God. I kissed Cleo. I kissed Jamie's girlfriend. I remember Jamie's "attention-seeking" comment. Maybe I was just being used. Or I wanted a bit of attention. I think I do have a slight crush on her, though. Mostly because she's so much cooler and more confident than me. She initiated it. I just sort of responded. Plus, there was the alcohol. I'd have kissed my weird cousin Hugh after that much champagne.

Okay, maybe I wouldn't go that far.

"Are you okay?" Dan says. "You look a bit…disgusted."

"Sorry, I was…thinking about something." I look up at him. I've got to make an effort. He can't do all this just for me to sit here in silence. I've got to put effort into people who matter. Not people who aren't even nice to me.

My phone buzzes.

"Sorry, it's my friend Gabi. Do you mind if I reply?"

"No, go ahead."

I've got about ten missed calls from home, so I also text Mom to say I'll be back in a few hours. Gabi immediately replies, inviting me to watch a DVD at Han's later. I've got a happy, buzzing feeling running through me, and when I put my phone away, Dan asks about Gabi and I just start talking, telling him about all our stupid private jokes and even the top-secret dances we made up to One Direction. He tells me about his friends, like Josh who drew a huge penis in weed killer on the school soccer field on senior prank day, and I start telling him about the girls at my school who brought a pig into class.

He's leaning back on his elbows and I'm lying on my front playing with blades of grass.

The sun beats down on us and the lake sparkles.

I feel like I could stay here forever.

Chapter 15

As we walk back down the hill again, Dan offers me his arm. We walk along like an old-fashioned couple. There's a warmness between us, and I want to squeeze his arm and tell him I'd like to spend as much time with him as possible. But a few worries surface as the lovely scenery of the picnic melts away and we get back into town. Are we a "thing" now? Have I implied I want to be a "thing"? Does that mean I have to tell him stuff, like I've started kissing random women?

It would be nice if I could just enjoy things without getting a flood of worry afterward. I look over at Dan. The sun is bouncing off his face and he looks completely relaxed as he swings the now much emptier basket in his other hand.

We get to my house and, with the worst timing in the world, Mom, Jeff, and Matthew are just getting out of the car after doing the weekly shopping. I drop Dan's arm and see Mom's eyes widen and her hands tense around a box of

Rice Krispies as she clearly decides in her head exactly why I stayed out last night.

"This is, um, Dan," I say, gesturing awkwardly in his direction. "This is Mom, Jeff, and Matthew."

Matthew blinks through his glasses. "Hello." Then he looks at me. "You look green."

"Thanks," I say, narrowing my eyes at him. I would usually kick him, but I figure Dan would think I was a bit immature. I'll kick him later.

"Hi, man," says Dan and holds out his hand. Matthew shakes it absentmindedly and then says, "I'm going to read my encyclopedia," and disappears into the house. I forgot to warn Dan my brother isn't normal.

Mom steps forward and shakes his hand. "Emma," she says. "That's probably better than 'Mom.'"

Dan laughs politely. "Can I give you a hand?"

Jeff says, in his stuttery, awkward way, that it's terribly kind of him to offer, but when I catch Jeff's eye, his face clouds over and it's obvious he's still annoyed about my late-night text. Dan and Mom go into the house laden with bags, and I sidle up to Jeff.

"Sorry. About, you know . . . last night and stuff."

He sighs. "It's fine, love. Just . . . I felt a bit taken for granted. You know I want you to enjoy this job, but give me a little more notice next time, eh?"

"Yep," I say, not looking at him and concentrating on picking up bags of oranges. Why does he have to be so frigging nice? I feel tears well up for the second time today. This hangover is making me weirdly emotional.

Dan stays for a long time, chatting away to my family, and Matthew even shows him his collection of flags from all the countries in the world. He comments pointedly that it's nice I'm not going out with a moron for a change. I think he overheard Kieran calling him a weirdo the one time I ever brought him over to the house.

We get forced into a family game of Taboo, instigated by Matthew, who by then has his friend over, Karen with the big eyes. I get stuck with Mom, who always overcomplicates everything. For instance, when I'm trying to describe the word "house," I say, "Thing you live in," and she starts going, "Studio? Maisonette? Igloo?" Then I say, "NO, just the normal one!" and she says, "Semi-detached?" and the timer runs out. She's no better when she has to describe the words, because she says stuff like, "You know, the little thing."

Jeff and Matthew are together and storm ahead, because their rounds sound like this:

Jeff: "He was the—"

Matthew: "HITLER."

Jeff: "The place w—"

Matthew: "LEBANON."

Dan does well with Karen with the big eyes, in spite of her unsettling habit of linking lots of her descriptions to death. Even though I'd usually rather spoon-feed myself vomit than play a family game with a boy I like, I have a really good time.

In the evening, when I'm going over to Han's, Dan is still there, so he comes with me. He doesn't seem fazed by being the only boy, and definitely makes a good impression by offering up the rest of the leftover food.

"Never turn down a free sausage," says Han wisely, and everyone nods in agreement. I try to ignore Gabi, who has started winking and pointing at Dan.

Later, when I get up to go to the bathroom, everyone

except Dan "needs it too" and they all file out of the room after me. Then everyone is whispering to me in the corridor about how much they like him. I'm enjoying all the attention, but at the same time it feels a bit pressured. I've only just met him, and people are already labeling us as "together." When the excitement dies down a bit, they go back into Han's room, but Gabi hangs back.

"It's good to see you, you punk."

"Sorry I've been crappy."

She grins. "Whatev. Come on. Danny's waiting."

While we're watching the movie, I sit between Dan's legs with his arms around me. My eyes start closing as the night before catches up with me, and I'm faintly aware of him moving his finger along my arm as if he's writing something.

It makes me think of bare legs touching.

Chapter 16

Walking along the river in the morning has a way of clearing your head. I breathe in and feel the cool, fresh air bombard every part of me. There are no clouds in the bright sky; it's gearing up to be another hot day.

I had the day after the picnic off, and Gabi came over. We sat outside in the yard talking and then in the evening watched DVDs in my room and ate our weight in cookies. Gabi's mom told her the other day that she should have a "life plan," so most of our conversation was taken up with trying, and failing, to think of one. Gabi's main ambition when she grows up is to be able to "stalk celebrities easily," but she hasn't worked out how that could be a job yet. She's gotten as far as trying to go on a reality show and "do stuff." I didn't ask what "stuff" was.

For my "life plan," we decided I'd use my new waitress skills to open a café somewhere cool, like Paris. It'd be nice if I could skip straight to that instead of having to go back to school first. But I suppose I can at least keep learning French.

She was hugely excited to hear about the party in the pool house and the weird games and the random kissing. But even as I was talking about it, I noticed I wasn't really mentioning Jamie.

Throughout the day Gabi tried to wrestle my phone from me to text Dan. I'm not sure what she was intending to say, but she is not to be trusted to do these things on her own. Matthew was in a good mood and brought us snacks, but that's also because he's a bit in love with Gabi. We let him sit on the floor and watch DVDs too. When Gabi made another attempt to text Dan, Matthew said, "Can you tell him I've got a list of questions for him?" and got a piece of paper out of his back pocket. I couldn't read most of it, but I could see that the first question was, *Did you take Latin?* Then Gabi and my brother collaborated, and when I got up to change the DVD, Dan was sent a message that said, `Hi sexy, can you name all the kings and queens of England?`

Dan brought it up a lot on our late shift together last night. Sometimes work is slow. It wasn't very busy, and the shift degenerated into a game of dares, which mostly involved eating things. I learned a valuable lesson: eating a teabag is not easy. It was all right for Dan, who just had to eat a flower.

I realize I'm walking along smiling now, remembering how ridiculous he looked. I don't care. Anyone who's around in the park to see me must be equally crazy to be up at this time. I feel like running. All the silly stuff about whether this is a "thing" or not doesn't matter. I like him, and he's making my summer job fun. I start to break into a run, not caring if I look like a grinning, sprinting lunatic.

My foot collides with something that feels like a soft branch. My main thoughts as I fly through the air and land flat on my face are:

1) This is why it is never a good idea to run.

2) What on earth is a "soft branch"?

3) OW.

I move up onto my knees and look behind me to see what I've tripped over.

Jamie is sitting up and staring at me. He's looking disheveled, and his eyes are only half-open. He's wearing suit pants and a crumpled shirt with the collar sticking up on one side.

"Do you mind?" he says, his voice sounding deeper than normal. "I was sleeping."

"On the ground, outside?"

He widens his eyes to wake himself up. "Yes."

I'm pleased to find him in a similar state to me when I woke up on his sofa.

"How did you end up out here?"

"I had a thing." He staggers to his feet and looks with surprise at a wine bottle clutched in his hand. "A thing with nice wine. I wish I remembered it."

I raise my eyebrows at him, really enjoying his pain. He shoots me a frown, but there's a hint of a smile there.

Jamie strolls beside me as I head to the castle. He doesn't seem to feel the need to say anything.

"You're not a fan of small talk, then," I say as the castle looms into view.

"I'm not." He smiles at me and we walk on in silence.

I feel the urge to annoy him for some reason. I look over expectantly until he reacts.

"What?" He frowns.

"Try some small talk," I say, like it's something really daring.

He sighs. "Fine. Mia, how's your"—he waves his hand as if he cannot possibly think of anything that my life would involve—"father?"

"Fine, I think. He lives in California. How's yours?"

"Deeply unhappy and extremely wealthy."

We continue through the grounds and start along the main driveway. He managed to wander quite a ways from the pool house. I wonder if he was on his own.

"Don't they mind you having all those parties? Julia told Andreas off for blowing his nose the other day because it would disturb the guests."

"I'm entertaining the offspring of the guests a lot of the time," he says dryly. "And I can usually smooth things over the next morning. But it is causing an amusing rift between my parents. Father periodically threatens to throw me out."

"What does Ju— I mean, your mom think?"

Our feet crunch on the stony path as he considers. I can tell his brain is working more slowly than usual.

"She says I'm blowing off steam before university."

We've reached the front of the castle. I hear a rolling noise above us, and a few seconds later Cleo appears at a window to the right of the huge pillars. Jamie looks upward, shielding his eyes and wincing, like the daylight pains him.

"Oh, you're alive." She smiles sarcastically.

"I've got an awful headache, if you'd mind not nagging."

She looks at him, unimpressed, and he blows a kiss at her. She slams the window shut.

Jamie takes a swig from the bottle and makes a face.

"You should have kept it chilled," I tell him.

He ignores me.

"You should do something nice for her."

He frowns at me, but still doesn't say anything.

"Something romantic."

"Don't be disgusting, Joseph."

"Okay, don't, then." I start through reception toward the restaurant, and he's still following me.

"What sort of thing?"

"A nice gesture."

"Buy her a horse?"

There's a chance he's not even kidding.

"No, something personal. Like, take her for a picnic or something."

"Is that what your boyfriend does?"

"Yes, it is, actually." I'm not sure why I said that. I thought I should defend Dan.

"How lovely," he says.

Cleo comes and sits at the bar for much of the day. She's flipping through a Cambridge prospectus, trying to pick a course. She doesn't mention Jamie, so I don't either. However, as it approaches three o'clock, he walks straight past both of us into the kitchen. He's holding a big wicker basket.

Cleo looks up only briefly, but then continues reading about philosophy. I follow Jamie in.

"What's the magic word?" Dan is saying, not looking up from the cutlery he's polishing.

Jamie rolls his eyes. "*Please* could you, you know, do the thing." He gestures at the basket.

"I'll see what we have." Dan catches my eye and gives me a little smile.

I'm clearing my last table when Jamie emerges, the picnic basket now much heavier.

"Come on," he says to Cleo, nodding toward the door.

She looks at him, her eyebrows raised.

"I'm going to feed you from a basket. It's romantic, apparently."

I look down at the table and smile to myself.

Cleo shuts the prospectus and sighs. "I'll come if I can bring Mia too."

Okay, that's a little weird.

"I can't," I say. "I'm busy this afternoon."

"No, you're not," says Cleo. "I heard you say earlier you had absolutely nothing to do."

I try inviting Dan to make things a bit less weird, but he's going to play rugby. Jamie doesn't seem bothered either way, and Cleo is fixing me with a look that is pretty hard to say no to.

"Okay," I say, confused. "That will be nice and not weird at all . . . I'll just change and get my stuff."

The grounds of Radleigh Castle make for a picturesque picnic setting. We sit by a ruined archway that was part of the old outer wall. The strict squares of the back lawns, with their straight paths, colorful flower beds, and elaborate fountain at the center, give way to uneven grass. The archway is on the edge of a hill, which looks down over miles of wild countryside with the river zigzagging through. It makes me wish I were here on my own, rather than sitting in on another couple's picnic.

Cleo has me on one side and Jamie on the other, and she conducts the conversation like an orchestra, the main part being her, with Jamie and me being brought in when she requires it. So from that point of view I don't feel like an awkward intruder, at least. More like a person shaking a tambourine occasionally.

Cleo's phone rings, and within about ten seconds she has called the person an "insufferable bitch" and wandered off to argue with her.

"Her mother," says Jamie.

He throws something at me that lands on the grass in front of me. It's the fifty-pence coin.

"What does it say?" he asks.

"Tails," I tell him.

He looks at me, and his gaze hovers momentarily over my lips.

"Shame," he says.

Chapter 17

The next day, Julia calls us all together for an announcement.

"In a week's time, we are hosting a very important event."

"Oh, a society wedding," Melanie whispers confidently. She had a few days off "sick" after the phone incident, but came back telling everyone emphatically how great she's feeling and that she and Simon are in a really, *really* good place.

"It is Desdemona's birthday," continues Julia.

"Right," whispers Dan. "What milestone age do you suppose she's reaching?"

"My daughter's fourteenth birthday," Julia says, "will be attended by her many friends and, of course, by their parents. I'll need extra people for serving drinks and a couple more than usual in the kitchen. Since it is not part of your contracted hours, you will get double pay. It *shall...*"

She raises her voice to quell the muttering that's started up about who's volunteering. "It *shall* go off without a hitch."

I'm on the late shift already on that day, so I head back to the kitchen and avoid the rush for the schedule. Dan follows me, telling me he won't be working the birthday. He's off for a few days on a mountain-biking trip.

Julia catches me on our way to start our shift.

"Speaking of birthdays, Mia, there's a family that's just arrived with a cake. Go collect it for them."

I go to the restaurant entrance and hear voices that I'm sure I know but can't quite place. Then I see the woman coming toward me. She has curly black hair, tanned skin, and is holding a cake box.

"Oh, hello… Don't I know you?" she says with a slight Spanish accent.

It's Kieran's mom. A cold, sickening feeling floods through me.

When Kieran comes through the door, his eyes go wide with shock, but he quickly looks down at his feet and coughs.

We'd become skilled at avoiding each other, and now we've been thrown together with no way out.

I wish it were socially acceptable to turn and run when you see people you don't like.

"Is this one of your friends, Kieran? I'm sure I recognize her."

Kieran mumbles, "Yeah," and appears to be finding his shoes fascinating.

"What's the holdup?" says Kieran's dad. He turns to me, obviously not remembering me at all. "Five bottles of Moët, please. We have the crypt room reserved—Saunders, for twenty."

91

The crypt is a private dining room that still has lots of the original castle stonework and arching ceilings, so people can pretend they are back in medieval times.

I can see other people arriving behind them. Then Jemima, Kieran's twelve-year-old sister, skips past.

"Hi, Mia," she says confidently.

"Um, I'm Mia. I've come to collect your cake," I say to his mom and then take it from her, trying not to show that my hands are shaking.

"Mia will be your waitress today." Julia suddenly appears in full-on lady-of-the-house mode with a gleaming smile. "Ask for anything you like and she will find a way." She puts her hand on my back and quite forcefully directs me to the kitchen.

It's a whole family affair, with grandparents, aunts, uncles, and cousins, and, worst of all, Kieran's friends Greg and Cooper. I have to serve them, but I don't look at them, not once, although I hear Greg snorting with laughter as I walk away. The kitchen is boiling, and I think I'm going to collapse if I don't go get some air. I announce I'm taking my break now, and I hear Dan asking if I'm okay as I hurry out the door.

I lean against the stone wall at the side of the terrace. If I smoked, this would be a good time to have a cigarette. As I'm thinking that, pieces of ash fall from above me, landing in my hair and on my nose. I look up and there's Jamie, leaning out a window with a cigarette hanging from his mouth.

"You look angry, Joseph." There's giggling from behind him.

"I'm fine."

I hear the crunch of heels on gravel and see Cleo approaching from the front of the castle.

"Ah," Jamie says through his cigarette, "darling." He takes it out of his mouth and pushes someone from behind so that she's also leaning out the window. She has curly brown hair in disarray and is wrapped in a bedsheet. "I'd like you to meet Patricia."

"I'm Persephone."

"As you wish."

Cleo strides up to me, ignoring him. "I'll need a gin and tonic," she says, her eyes flicking upward before registering my face. "What's wrong with you?"

"Kieran's here," I blurt out.

She considers this for a moment. Then she sweeps my bangs across my forehead and takes a few strands of hair out of my clip so they hang around my face. "Well, it's a good thing you look fucking hot," she says. Then she undoes the top button on my shirt. "I'll take care of the rest."

I have no idea what she means, but I go back in feeling different. Calmer. When I give Greg his dessert, I look straight at him and raise my eyebrows, daring him to laugh again. He's at the angle where he'd be able to see the top of my boobs, and I see him look. His eyes move quickly back up to my face and I deliberately look disgusted. He turns pink and starts muttering to Cooper as I walk away. I come out of the crypt and into the main restaurant. Through the conservatory I can see Cleo and Jamie in deep conversation.

I turn back and walk straight into Kieran, who's walking across the restaurant toward the restrooms. He goes straight past me. Cleo moves through the courtyard and past the window, aiming to head him off. I peer through the restaurant door into the corridor where the bathrooms are, trying to see what's going on without being seen myself. Cleo

93

is talking to him, though I can't hear what she's saying, and twisting a strand of hair around her fingers. Then she leans in and whispers something in his ear. Kieran's eyebrows raise and he looks at her and grins.

I remember that look. The cold panic that's been underlying all my thoughts since he walked in is replaced by anger. So he just carries on as usual. He isn't paranoid. He doesn't stop at every moment and wonder what people will think of him.

Cleo pushes open the door behind him and he goes in. I don't know if he knows that it's the girls' room. Cleo lets the door close and walks back into the courtyard.

"Mia!" It's Julia. "You've already had your break. The table needs clearing."

Grudgingly, I head back into the crypt and start loading myself up with plates. Most people left the cake in the end.

Suddenly there's a scream. Dezzie comes running in, followed by Cleo. Dezzie has tears running down her face.

"What's the matter?" says Julia, running over.

"It was horrible!" sobs Dezzie. "He was naked and...doing things." She turns and buries her face in Cleo's chest.

Then Kieran comes running through the door. He's obviously just dressed in a hurry, because his shirt buttons don't match up and he's wearing only one shoe.

"Wait, wait! It's not...I thought—"

He sees Cleo standing there with her arm around Dezzie and his mouth drops open.

"You...You said—"

Kieran's dad, his face bright red, stands up. "What on earth is going on?" he blusters, sending a shower of spit everywhere.

94

Cleo speaks in a calm, clear voice. "I'm so sorry, Mr. Saunders," she says. "I know it's your son's birthday, but really, self-abuse in a public place is just not appropriate. I think he might have a problem." Suppressed giggles go around the table.

One of the grannies asks loudly, "He's done a what?"

"Something about a goose," another one replies.

"Kieran!" his dad thunders as his mom mutters, "Oh dear," into her napkin.

"I WASN'T!" Kieran shrieks. His voice bounces off the stone walls.

"It's just not something that someone as young as Dezzie should have to see," says Cleo.

Dezzie shakes her head plaintively.

"Mia!" Julia snaps into action. "I said clear the table. I'll deal with this."

After some hushed conversation between Julia and Kieran's dad outside the room, the Saunders party is ushered out. His mom looks mortified as the rest of them whisper and the grannies still talk about the goose. Kieran's just walking along in stunned silence. He looks back at me once, the only time he's actually met my eye, and I shrug.

But as he gets into the courtyard, I see a figure beckon him over. It's Jamie. What does he want? I go to the door and crane my head around to see.

"Hey."

I jump violently and nearly drop my plates.

"Whoa, sorry," says Dan, and takes some of them off me. "What's going on?"

"He's my ex. He…We…" I trail off. I can't work out whether I'm delighted or severely panicked by all of this.

"Yeah, he went to my school," Dan says, and then lowers his head nearer to mine. "Not a nice guy."

He knows, then.

I look away from him. With Dan it's all easy conversation and banter and making fun of each other. Right now it's like he's seeing behind it all, seeing deeper. If I meet his eye, then I'm telling him something real about me. For a moment, I get that familiar anger when people know things about me that I can't control.

I told Cleo, though. I know her even less than I know Dan. But I just wanted her to think I was interesting. I want Dan to think I'm put together and confident and don't make mistakes. It's like I can put up these screens and show people what I want them to see, but then they wobble and I know that eventually they'll come crashing down and everyone will see what's behind. Just me.

I look into Dan's eyes.

"Don't worry," he says and looks around to make sure Julia's not in sight. Then he kisses me on the lips, and I sink in to him for a second. We move apart and I smile at him, but only one thought is hammering at my brain.

What was Jamie up to?

Chapter 18

The week leading up to Dezzie's birthday is punctuated by people in the courtyard measuring things and Julia saying things like, "The replica night sky will go there," but other than that, things at Radleigh Castle are pretty much the same.

Cleo comes to see me at the end of some of my shifts, which still makes me feel a bit disloyal to the other waiters, but I feel like I owe her after the Kieran incident. I tried to thank her but she just waved my words away, and I didn't mention it after that.

Gabi said that the news got around pretty quickly and Kieran was getting lots of flack. She knows what really happened, obviously, but she wasn't as excited as I thought she'd be when I told her. She said, "Oh. So why did she do that for you?"

I didn't really have an answer for that. I said that maybe Cleo just liked me.

Gabi said, "Well, you did make out with her."

There was a tense silence before she slipped back into normal Gabi chat mode. She's clearly a little grumpy that I'm making new friends.

On a couple of occasions Jamie has come in with Cleo, and I've watched him for any sign of what he might have said to Kieran. But he doesn't seem to be acting any differently around me. Maybe it was nothing. Just a random conversation. Once he saw me watching and we looked at each other for a moment. I still get that nervous feeling when he does that. Cleo interrupted and my attention went back to her. But I could still feel Jamie's gaze on me.

The shifts are kept fun by whatever silly games we think up to play, and we hear pieces of gossip from the pool house, where the games have far more serious consequences—for the losers, anyway. Jamie got some guy to gamble away a large chunk of his parents' money on online poker. And they started a rumor that some local landowner had an overly friendly relationship with his dogs.

One night Jamie, his friend Freddie, Cleo, and her friends Nish and Effy come in for a meal. Their raucous conversation, emphasized by Effy's loud, dirty laugh, keeps me far more entertained than the forced politeness of many of the guests. I get invited to join them after my shift. At first I'm reluctant, but it's hard to say no to Cleo, and Jamie pours me a drink and points to the seat next to him. I sip my drink and feel shy and boring next to the loudness. Cleo holds the attention of the table expertly, and the others pipe up with funny comments. I feel like I'm at a tennis match as I turn from person to person and watch the words fly back and forth. Suddenly Freddie turns to me.

"Is this one a mute?" he drawls.

I feel the redness creep over my cheeks.

Jamie jumps in, a tinge of annoyance to his voice. "I expect she's bored stiff by your incessant talk about your father's money."

Freddie laughs, but eyes Jamie warily.

"Anyway...," says Cleo, and the conversation starts up again.

Jamie turns to me and speaks quietly, so as not to get the attention of the whole table.

"So. Mia. How's your mother?"

I lean in toward him. "Are you attempting small talk again?"

He smiles. "I am."

This warmth between us isn't something I've ever felt talking to Jamie. And I'm sure he'll ruin it by saying something obnoxious. But for now I'm happy to sit here, talking quietly against the backdrop of shrieks and laughter.

Dan's parents have gone away on vacation, so the night before he goes off on his mountain-biking trip, he has people over. He told me I could bring people too, so I went on Facebook for the first time in about two weeks and invited Gabi and the girls and Max.

Dan's friends introduce us to a game called Ring of Fire, in which a pack of cards is laid facedown in a ring and everyone takes turns picking one card. Each suit means a different type of dare or tells you how much of your drink you have to down. I get both mocked—for being unable to think of a single flavor of chips when someone chose a category card—and respected, if that's the right word, for being surprisingly good at rapping. The girls note some potential hotties among Dan's friends, and Ring of Fire soon dissolves into groups of people chatting and dancing.

I bump into Dan on the stairs.

"ARE YOU HAVING FUN?" he shouts.

"YES!" I reply, a huge grin on my face.

He starts talking to me and our heads are close in an attempt to hear each other better. I inhale his fresh, sweet smell.

He quickly realizes I can't hear a word he's saying. He grabs my hand and pulls me to his bedroom. His friend Josh calls after us, "Stay safe, kids!" and a couple of other people whoop. As Dan shuts the door, he raises his eyebrows at me and laughs awkwardly. We hear a few more cheers through the door.

I see his bed out of the corner of my eye. For a moment it seems everything distorts and the bed grows to take up the whole room. Could something happen? I imagine launching myself at him and immediately cringe. I'd definitely need more wine to do that.

I sit down on his bed and say, "Well, this is nice."

"Yes!" he says, politely ignoring the fact that I'm behaving a little like someone's mother.

He sits down next to me and I have this sudden urge to just fall off the bed to break the tension. I bounce up and down on the mattress. I do not know why.

"Springy," I say. Again, I do not know why.

"Yes." He laughs. He's very close to me. I am trying desperately to think of something to say that doesn't reference the fact that we're on his bed. He's smiling shyly at me. I look at his dimples. And the way his eyes sparkle.

He just lets his smile take over his face. Maybe I *do* want to reference the fact that we're on his bed.

I think maybe I'm staring too much, and I look up at the walls. Lots of posters of motorcycles, including one with a naked girl draped across it. At last, I have something to mock him for.

"She seems nice. Is she your friend?" I point at the wall.

"Hey, I bet your wall is covered in oily men!" he protests.

I go to poke him in the stomach and he grabs my arms. I wriggle away, and it descends into one of those play-fights where you laugh so much you feel like you can't breathe. When I catch his eye, there's a flutter of excitement between us. It's not hard to figure out where this is leading.

I grab his wrists and push him backward. I feel him let me.

We're still for a moment, and for some reason I almost start to laugh. He looks like he's suppressing a smile too. I lean in and he grabs the back of my head.

The first kiss is forceful, our lips pushing together. Then we kiss more lightly, every so often feeling our tongues briefly touch. I have my hands on his neck and in his hair.

Suddenly images of Cleo flicker through my head, the way she crawled up Jamie's body in her lingerie.

I slip down and then slowly move my way up him, grazing my body against him so he'll feel friction all the way up through his clothes. When our faces are level he looks surprised, but not in a bad way. We're on the edge of something exciting. Of something changing. And the look that passes between us says we want it to happen.

He pulls me in closer; then the door swings open and one of his friends crashes in.

I leap up and Dan scrambles into a cross-legged position. I'm kneeling up on the bed and pat the mattress.

"Just testing this," I say quickly.

"Springy," says Dan.

"Nothing sexual," I add. Sometimes I shouldn't be allowed to talk.

His friend is really drunk, so isn't even listening. He staggers to the bed and lies back on it. Dan and I look at each other over him.

"Back to the party?" asks Dan.

I smile at him, consider for a moment, and nod.

When Gabi and I get picked up much later, Dan and I say good-bye more shyly than usual, but I feel like we're still both suppressing a smile.

Chapter 19

I arrive at work for Desdemona's big night. Even though I knew Julia was going all out, I'm still surprised at the transformation. There's a canopy over the courtyard now, threaded through with twinkling lights to look like a sky full of stars. Ice sculptures and a champagne fountain extend the glittering effect all around. A violin quartet in the corner plays throughout the evening and makes the hubbub and chatter of the party sound musical.

Dezzie is wearing a white and silver nineteen-twenties-style flapper dress, complete with a wide headband, and is drifting around seeming spectacularly blasé about the whole thing.

I'm on wine duty, weaving my way in and out of floppy-haired fourteen-year-olds and balding men in black tie, girls in fabulous dresses, and startlingly coiffured women. And Jamie. His shirt collar is open, his bow tie already undone around his neck. He's leaning against one of the archways. I'd never tell him, but he looks really good. The other men, with their done-up collars and bow ties nestling under their chins, look uptight and pompous in comparison. Jamie looks like he doesn't care. Like he could blow the whole polite facade of the party apart if he wanted to.

"Excellent job, Joseph. Fill them up."

"More wine, sir?" I say sarcastically.

"Not drinking." He holds up a glass of water.

"Really?"

"Babysitting," he says, and right on cue, a group of boys moves our way.

"Seriously, dude, Dezzie's bangin'," one of them whispers, and then is vigorously elbowed by another who's seen Jamie watching. The group falls silent.

"Please continue, Jonty. You were discussing my sister?"

"No, no, I, um..."

"Good. Because if I hear that you are, I'll tell your little friends what I found on your Internet history."

The boy turns white, and his friends burst into guffaws as they shepherd him away.

Jamie glares after him. For a second I get a flash of something he genuinely feels.

"What does he have on his Internet history?"

"No idea," says Jamie. "When do you finish?"

"Not for hours. I didn't know when everything would end, so my stepdad's sort of on standby."

"I'll take you home."

I start to think of a reason to say no, but he's gone. I get this urge to follow him, but at the same time I'm relieved. I can't really work out what I'm thinking. It's like glimpsing something real about him makes me want to know more and get closer. But then the idea of getting close to Jamie fills me with instinctive, and probably totally reasonable, panic.

While there's no one around, I decide to text Dan. Just so he knows I'm thinking about him while he's away. I wonder if I should text Cleo as well. She's just gone to the Seychelles for a family vacation. She said she was dreading two weeks alone with her parents and sister.

"You'll find stuff to distract you," I told her. I can picture her walking around, doing whatever the hell she wants, probably being followed by a bunch of drooling guys like she is here.

"Yeah," she said, not really listening. We were in her room—well, the room she's taken over in Radleigh Castle. Better than staying at her school over the summer, she says. It's a tower room, so the walls curve around in a circle. It has an arched window with a sill big enough to sit on; a huge wall mirror with an ornate wooden frame, which is apparently hundreds of years old; and a four-poster bed. So, you know, just your average hotel room.

Cleo tossed a few bikinis into her Louis Vuitton suitcase and then went over to the mirror and sighed. "It's a hundred four degrees, apparently."

"God, how awful..." I shook my head. She caught my eye in the reflection and we shared a smile. She went back to examining herself.

"Keep an eye on him," she said, putting on lip gloss and then pressing her lips together. "I don't care what he does so long as I know."

I frowned. "Yeah, sure. I mean, if you really want to know."

"Good," she said, shaking out her hair and turning away

105

from the mirror. "So, your hair." She marched over to me. "What color are you going for?"

I'd told her I wanted a change. I've never dyed my hair. Well, except for the time Gabi and I decided we wanted blond streaks and ended up looking like birds had pooped on our heads. We don't speak of that.

"Red." Jamie appeared at the door. "You should dye it red."

Cleo didn't look up from her packing.

"I got you a going-away present, darling," Jamie said, moving into the room.

She continued to ignore him, so he threw a small velvet box across the room to me before leaving and closing the door.

"Do you want..." I held it out to her.

"What is it?" she said, with a note of exasperation.

I opened it. It was a necklace. Gold with a pearl drop. "It's... It's lovely," I said.

She took it from me, looked at it for a second, and then snapped the box shut.

A few hours later, when the taxi came to pick her up, I saw she was wearing the necklace.

I head to the bar, where I've left my phone out of sight, and wonder what I should text to Cleo. And whether she would mind me getting a lift with Jamie.

I shake my head. I'm overreacting. It's getting into his car, not his bed. And I'm not going to, anyway. I get my phone out and there's a text there from Dan saying he misses me.

I look up and see Jamie through the window. He's talking to a woman who's probably Mom's age, and she keeps laughing and touching his chest. He's wearing a half smile as he talks to her. Then he looks over. Right at me. He kisses the air slowly.

106

Just don't kiss him.

My conversation that night with Cleo floods back. *Just by kissing.* An involuntary tingle goes through me.

I stare back at him and mouth, "Seriously?"

He mouths it back, making a stupid face. And then he turns to the woman. But I wait, and he looks past her, right at me again. Slowly, he looks me up and down. His eyes hover momentarily over my chest and then drift farther down, and it's like I can feel fingers brushing over me. His gaze moves over my legs, and then he looks straight into my eyes again and I shiver.

I delete my reply to Dan and open a new message.

`Hi Jeff, am getting a lift. You can go to bed!x`

Chapter 20

I'm busy all night, which is probably a good thing, because it stops me from thinking about the ride home. A floppy-haired boy named Spencer follows me around asking for refills until he vomits down his front and passes out. I leave him in the hands of his friends, who begin to film themselves drawing on him.

One of the bald men, who is possibly Spencer's dad, also follows me around, shouting that I'm his "favorite" before falling into a bush. I find it amusing that in normal life he probably runs a company or something.

I'm just going to get a fresh bottle of wine when someone pokes me in the back. I turn around and there's a large old woman sitting on a chair at the edge of the courtyard. She's cloaked in silk and looks a little like an angry toad.

"Would you like my strawberry titty?"

"I'm...I'm sorry?"

"This thing." I realize she's holding out one of the

miniature strawberry-and-cream desserts in little jars that we'd handed out. She taps the jar with her finger.

"Um, no, thank you. I'm working, so I probably shouldn't."

I feel an arm slip around my shoulder.

"Awfully impolite of you to turn down Aunt Beryl's strawberry titty," says Jamie.

"Oh, okay." I hold my hand out, thanking the lady while trying desperately to keep a straight face and not catch Jamie's eye.

I hold the dessert up to him, speaking quietly. "I don't want it. Too small."

"Very kind of you, Aunt Beryl," says Jamie, flashing her a huge fake smile.

"Don't give me that crap, you little rogue," she snaps, every word sending ripples down her chins. "Are you still as useless as ever?"

"I certainly am," he replies, nodding deferentially at her.

She rises to her feet, and the chair gives a creak of relief. As she starts to shuffle off, she turns to me.

"You hold on to your panties with that one, girl. There's no hope for him."

Luckily she doesn't wait for me to respond. We both watch her go for a moment.

"You can take your arm off me now," I say.

He slides his hand away, deliberately dragging his fingers across my back. I squirm, trying to conceal the shiver that just went over my skin.

"Has anyone ever told you how creepy you are?"

"No," he says, smiling. "Come upstairs. I want to show you something."

"What?" I say suspiciously.

"Not my penis," he says loudly. "I wish you'd stop asking."

A group of women nearby shoot us wide-eyed stares. I start moving glasses around on a table to look busy.

"Come on. You must be due for a break."

His eyes shine wickedly at me. My urge to know more about him is too strong, and I know I'm going to follow.

"Okay, but if it's anything weird, I'm leaving."

I follow him to the door in the corner of the courtyard that leads into reception, and he heads for the wooden door that I saw on my interview day. It opens onto a spiral stone staircase. In one direction the steps descend into darkness, probably to the network of secret passageways. But Jamie starts climbing upward. I lose count of the steps and my legs start to ache as we near the top. Jamie pushes against another heavy wooden door and then holds it open for me.

I walk through and realize I'm at the top of one of the four towers. The hot days have kept the evenings warm, but there is more of a breeze up here than down in the courtyard.

The panoramic view is made even more dramatic by the moonlight. It's dizzying. Black outlines of trees. Blue fields. The sparkling lights from the town.

"How do you like the view?"

I look around for Jamie and see him sitting on the edge of the turret, facing outward. My stomach lurches. He could so easily fall.

"Not bad," I say, staying by the door.

He swings his legs back around so that he's facing me. The breeze is moving through his hair. He grins at me and then grabs a cigarette from a pack lying on the wall and lights it.

110

"So whose wife are you after tonight, then?" I cross my arms. "Or will you just be encouraging someone to gamble away all their money?"

"Not tonight." He looks at me steadily.

I watch him expectantly. His expression is almost defiant, like I shouldn't be able to force an explanation out of him. We face off for a moment, and then he laughs and turns to see the view.

"I've been finding myself less bored lately." He keeps his eyes turned away.

I look at him from the side. He's frowning in thought, but giving nothing away about what those thoughts might be. And there's something at the edges drawing me in. Making me frustrated because I can't figure him out. Does he really do all this just because he's bored?

There's the sound of the door thudding shut and the patter of footsteps. Jamie looks over.

"Desmond."

Dezzie is walking over to us. I smile at her and she stares back.

"What's she doing here?"

"Don't be grumpy, Desmond. Mia's going to sing you happy birthday."

"I'm not," I say hurriedly.

"Good. That would be weird," says Dezzie. She leans forward and plucks a cigarette from Jamie's pack and runs toward something I hadn't spotted before—a wooden shelter that's been propped up in a ramshackle way against the turreted wall. She disappears inside.

Jamie jumps up with a flash of annoyance on his face. I follow him over to the shelter. We're on the part of the tower nearest to the courtyard, so can hear a hum of chatter from the party below.

We hear the click of a lighter, and then a small puff of smoke billows out from the shelter. Jamie stoops and looks into the entrance.

"Desmond, don't be an idiot," he says.

"I learned it from you," she replies evenly.

"It's different," he says, frowning.

She pokes her head out and blows smoke in his face and then retreats back inside. He follows her.

I'm intrigued, despite Dezzie's hostile glares, and I hover at the entrance.

"Come in, for God's sake," snaps Jamie, still clearly rattled by Dezzie's smoking. He pats a cushion next to him. This is some sort of den. There are piles of books and comics in the corner, some dusty plastic boxes that look like they contain toys, and a shoebox that, when I peer at it, I see has *Hands off* written on it in Sharpie.

He sees me looking. "The profits of smuggling. Chocolate, mostly."

"So this is a Radleigh secret, then?" Despite really wanting to not think it's cool, I do.

"Not anymore," Dezzie sighs.

"Pa discovered it a few years ago," says Jamie through his cigarette. "He knows where to look for us now, so we don't usually have too long."

Dezzie flicks on a flashlight and bathes the whole place into a warm yellow light. I realize that the sloping roof wall is covered in chalk. There are games of hangman, scrawled messages, an unflattering cartoon of a man's face with *Dick* written under it. A heart with the letters *J* and *C* inside.

112

I suddenly register a detail I saw when I first sat down— empty wine bottles. Next to them, burned-down candles. Jamie must have brought Cleo up here.

With a jolt, I realize that I have no way of telling the time. My fifteen minutes are probably up. But then the sound of the door opening, much more forcefully this time, makes Jamie and Dezzie both freeze.

Dezzie's hand clutching the cigarette waves in panic. I lean over, grab it from her, and jam it into my mouth. The crunching footsteps stop outside the entrance to the den. I duck down and come slowly out to face him.

Richard Elliot-Fox definitely has elements of Jamie about him. His posture is brimming with easy confidence, and I can tell through his shirt that he's tanned and muscular, even if he does have a little middle-aged belly going on. His thick blond hair is carefully crafted into ripples, with none of Jamie's messiness. And instead of those deep, dark eyes, his eyes are small and mean.

"Hello!" I wave cheerily. I point to the cigarette in my hand. "Smoke break!"

Jamie has followed me out. He stands next to me, and when our eyes meet, he smiles at me gratefully. Dezzie emerges from the den, smiling sweetly at her father.

"I would appreciate it if you wouldn't indulge your filthy habit around my daughter," he says icily. "And that goes for you too," he snaps at Jamie. He turns to Dezzie, and his face softens slightly, although his eyes remain cold. "My darling, if you could bring yourself to put in an appearance at your own special occasion, Aunt Beryl has no children of her own and enough money to fund the rest of your education."

113

Dezzie rolls her eyes and trudges past him.

He waves his hand dismissively at me. "Aren't you supposed to be handing out sausages or something?"

"I am." I nod politely. I stub out the cigarette and Jamie takes it from me, clearly realizing that I don't know where to put it.

As I walk back across the tower roof, I hear Richard's low, cold voice continuing, although I can't make out what he's saying. When I reach the door, I turn back for a moment. Jamie is stony and silent; then, in the middle of Richard's speech, he gives a loud yawn.

Richard leans forward, pointing a finger right in Jamie's face, and even from here I can see Jamie's expression darken.

Jamie rolls down the window as we speed along the road back into town. He drives a flashy sports car, of course, but I have no idea what kind. Silver and fast.

"You didn't bring your gorilla tonight, then."

"No, he's off mountain biking," I reply without thinking. "I mean, just call him Dan...And he's not mine."

"I thought you were with 'Dan'?"

"We're not..." I pause. I don't know what we are really. "I like his silly jokes."

Jamie looks like that's the most appalling thing he's ever heard.

"Just because you haven't, like, laughed at or told a joke in your life," I mutter.

Jamie gives me a look—a frown with a lot of pouting.

"Oh, I'm sorry. Do you actually do anything besides pout at people?"

"Why are you sorry?"

"Okay, I didn't go to, like, finishing school, so—"

"If you had been to 'like, finishing school,' you would at least have learned to speak properly."

"I don't care if I don't speak properly."

"Why not?"

"Because I'm normal."

He lets out a small nasal laugh.

"Ooh, was that a tiny laugh?" I say in a mock-excited voice, and he smiles—a real, unplanned smile.

"No."

There's a silence for a while, and then we're approaching the traffic circle near my house. I tell him it's the first exit. He slows the car to a halt in the middle of the road, but it hardly matters since the whole town is deserted.

"Do you like swimming?"

"Um, I suppose."

"Let's go swimming."

He revs the engine and we move off again. He misses the first exit.

"Wait, I—I don't have my stuff..." He swings past the other exits and back onto the road we came down. We're heading back to Radleigh Castle.

Chapter 21

Just swimming. That's fine, isn't it? It's exercise. Exercise
that means I'm standing next to Jamie in my underwear.

I'm struggling to trace back the steps that led to this.
The castle was silent when we walked past on our way
from the parking lot. The party ended at one, and as Jamie
walked me to his car, I saw Julia being firm in ejecting any
stragglers. Any of the guests who overdid it would by now
be feeling very sorry for themselves in the back of their
parents' cars, hoping vomit doesn't stain a dinner jacket.
There's no one else around.

I scrunch my feet on the plastic coping around the pool.
My arms are firmly crossed over my body. The lights in
the main house are all off, and it feels like I'm completely
surrounded by darkness.

"I'm freezing."

"Get in, then. It's heated."

"Do you bring lots of girls back to your pool?"

"Yes," he says and launches off the side in a clean dive into the water.

I can't make myself jump in, so I go to the metal ladder in the corner and start climbing in backward.

"God, you're going about as fast as my grandmother."

His hands appear at my waist and pull me back. I slip down into the water. He brings his head close to mine, so he's whispering into my ear. "Do you want to know what I do to every girl I bring back here?"

I don't say anything and swallow, trying to slow my breathing.

"She'll hold on here." He puts his hands over mine, closing them around the handrail.

"I'm behind her."

I can feel his mouth on the back of my neck.

"Her breathing gets faster."

He moves closer. His body is touching mine. I feel electricity running up and down my legs.

"She bites her lip."

The tingling is centered now within me, pulsing.

"She cries out for more."

The feeling rises with every breath and I turn my head. Our lips are an inch apart.

And Dan's face comes crashing into my thoughts.

A horrible, guilty feeling weighs down on me and I duck down under the water. As I sink, Jamie's stomach and shorts and legs flash past me, and the urge to pull him on top of me throbs everywhere.

I swim past his legs and away, coming up to the surface on the other side of the pool.

"There. I've done my swimming," I say, trying to keep my voice level.

He laughs. "And now Scrabble?"

For the second time in two weeks, I wake up on Jamie's sofa. He offered me the bed, but considering he probably meant with him in it, I insisted on the sofa. He wakes me up at six thirty and I mumble that I don't have work. His response is to tap the side of my face with his hand until I open my eyes.

"What?" I say as a fresh wave of guilt breaks over me.

He nods toward the door. "Put some clothes on and come outside."

I sit up groggily and get to my feet. "I am wearing clothes," I say. I follow him out and am hit by a breeze that reminds me that by "clothes" I mean only Jamie's sweater and boxers.

Another fresh, clear day.

The air outside is crisp, and the grass around the pool is damp. I see streaks of pink reflected in the water and then I look up and gasp. Ruffles of pink cloud cover the sky, shot through with flashes of blue. The castle is a majestic silhouette, and the trees twist in shadowy shapes behind it.

I follow Jamie's dark figure as he makes his way to the grounds at the back of the castle. He lies back on the grass. I lie down next to him. And we look up.

All I can see is the sky. I let it overwhelm me and switch off all the thoughts and worries in my brain. I feel Jamie shift next to me, moving closer. And then he takes my hand.

• • •

118

That's how it began.

My double life.

In the day, I worked and fell easily into being with Dan. Every time I told myself we were just friends, someone would comment how good we were together. After a while, I stopped protesting.

Then, at two in the morning, I'd swim.

Sometimes I'd go to Jamie's party first. Sometimes he'd pick me up. Either way, I'd find myself there.

At first we would just swim, sharing a few words at the end of each lap. And then talking would take over. We'd talk quietly and close together, so as not to alert anyone from Radleigh. He'd let his sarcasm drop, just for a bit, and I'd see something real.

It was like I was chasing those moments. A glimpse into his childhood. Or what scared him. Or what he really cared about.

But there was something else keeping me there. Something dangerous and exciting because it hadn't been put into words. Each time we'd meet, we'd take it a little bit further. Not in what we did, but in what we said. Finding words that painted pictures of what we wanted to do.

Turning those words into actions was all I could think about.

Jamie Elliot-Fox is toxic.

That was still to come.

Chapter 22

I'm walking along the road near my house with Dan. Every so often our hands brush against each other. We're quoting lines from *The Office*.

When we get near my house, but not quite in view of the windows, I stop and softly punch him on the arm. His face is illuminated by the pool of light from a streetlamp. I realize I'm standing in the shadows.

"S'yalater," I say, which we've started saying instead of good-bye.

"S'yalater," he says.

He leans in to kiss me and then stops when he realizes I've already started turning to go.

I turn back. "Oh!"

"No, it's fine," he says quickly.

"No, I..." I step toward him. We kiss once on the lips.

Watching him walk away, I feel a wave of uneasiness. I

stand there, hidden from my house by a bush. I'm prolonging the moment of decision. I walk one way and go into my house. My parents know I'm there, and so there'll be no swimming. I go the other way, and walk back to Radleigh.

I suppose there is a third option: I could live in this bush.

That is actually pretty tempting. I could make a bed out of leaves, be friends with the mice and birds...I bet mice and birds don't invite you to go naughty swimming with them. If they did, then they would wear those modest swimsuits that Victorian people wore and it would all be very innocent.

While I'm thinking this, and possibly going insane, the decision is made for me, because Mom appears and scares the living crap out of me.

I scream. She screams and throws the trash bag she's holding across the road.

"What are you doing?" I shriek, despite my being the one who was hiding behind the bush and despite it being completely obvious that she's putting out the garbage. She eyes me warily as she picks up the bag.

"Bedtime, Mia. I think you've had a late enough night."

I'm lying in bed, staring at my alarm clock. I watch the numbers change. It's been forty-six minutes since I heard Mom's door close.

I move my legs up and down against the sheets. I'm still wearing my work stuff. Static crackles between my tights and the duvet as I carefully slide out of bed.

I never thought I would actually be arranging pillows in my bed to look like a person. I feel like I'm in a teen drama and, next episode, I'm going to be sneaking a boy in through my window or learning that drugs are bad.

As I walk slowly down the stairs, every tiny creak sounds deafening. My breathing sounds like a train going past.

I remember at the last minute to go out the back door; otherwise I'll trigger the security light.

I go along the river, rather than the road, so it's less likely anyone will see me. It's so dark I can't even see my own feet as I walk. I use my phone as a flashlight. I'm so excited by the nighttime mission that I don't stop to think that walking along the river at night could be incredibly dangerous.

As I approach the pool house, I realize I haven't even texted Jamie to let him know I'm on my way. Will he just be expecting me? More importantly, will he reference the fact that I have just sneaked out of my house and walked through the pitch black to get here? I'm hoping that my desperate behavior can just go uncommented on.

He looks at me curiously when he opens the door. Or it could be sleepily. He's rubbing his eyes and wearing a T-shirt and boxers, so I think I might have got him out of bed.

I jump inside before he has the chance to say anything. "Can we stay in? I don't feel like swimming."

He steps back to let me in and points toward his bedroom. "In there."

"What's in there?"

"My sex dungeon," he says and walks over to the kitchen, ruffling his hair. I go over, but pause at the door. You can never be totally sure with him.

"There's also a TV and a selection of movies," he continues, taking a bag out of the cupboard. "So it's up to you."

"Well, seeing how I've left my whip at home, I think I'll go with the movie."

He raises his eyebrows at me and gets out a saucepan.

He's making something in the kitchen, but calls through that I can find pajamas in the dresser. I inspect his room. Despite the nights I've spent in the pool house, I've never been in here. The TV is enormous and takes up most of the wall opposite the bed, which is also enormous. I peel back the duvet. Silk sheets.

I hear popping from the kitchen and realize what he's doing. I change quickly into a T-shirt and shorts and get into the bed. I set the alarm on my phone for five. That should give me enough time to sneak back home before anyone wakes up. Then Jamie arrives at the door with a bowl of freshly made popcorn.

He puts the bowl on the bed and takes off his T-shirt. I feel a thrill rising in my chest and look away from him. I know it's the same as seeing him in his swimming trunks, but being in his bed feels more risky. And exciting.

It feels less so when he tells me to move over and not to hog the popcorn.

We watch *Casablanca*. At first we're sitting separately, me with my knees drawn up to my chest and him lounging back on a pillow. At some point he puts his arm behind me and I slide backward. I end up with my head on his chest. I watch his stomach muscles move with the rise and fall of his chest. By the end of the film, his arm is around me. Just before I drift off to sleep, I think, *This is what it could be like*. Not sneaking around. Just being together.

Chapter 23

"I don't get it at all," says Mom. "If you're going to go off with someone else, then just break up with him."

"In her mind, she might think she's doing the right thing," says Jeff. "If she keeps it secret, no one gets hurt."

"Because it won't all come out in the end..." Mom shakes her head. "She's being a selfish idiot."

"We are inherently selfish beings," Matthew pipes up from behind his book.

I aim a kick at him under the table.

"Mia!" says Mom, seeing the kick. "It's enough that you're sitting there being a thoughtless cow, but what the hell."

I don't look at her and poke the peas on my plate with my fork.

"Don't you have an opinion?"

"No," I mutter. "I don't care about your crappy friends and their sad lives."

Mom glares at me. "Is there a reason for this mood?"

"I'm tired."

She nags at me for a while before I can escape to my room. I take my phone out of my sleeve and start plotting how I can get to the pool house tonight. I could say I was going to Gabi's... My thumb hovers uneasily over her name on my phone. I haven't told her about the swimming yet. Obviously I will. We tell each other everything. She's just been getting so excited planning double dates for her and Max with me and Dan. She loves Dan.

My eyes switch focus to the twisted leather bracelet on my wrist. Dan got it for me on his biking trip. Like the bell on a clock, the thought strikes me again. Dan.

I close my eyes and wait for it to fade away. Since he got back from his trip, he's had his cousin staying with him and so he's been a little preoccupied. He keeps saying at work that we haven't had a chance to really see each other since he's been back. I think guiltily that it's pretty lucky that he hasn't noticed what I've been up to.

She should just break up with him.

What's wrong with me? I really, really like Dan.

Imaginary Mom pops up in my head. *If you really like him, then don't lead him on.*

But if I break up with Dan, then I'm just left with this weird... thing with Jamie. Who has a girlfriend anyway.

Having a boyfriend isn't everything, Mi. You need to know you'd be okay on your own.

Imaginary Mom is really annoying.

Oh, easy for you to say, Mom. You went out with Dad when you were my age and he went and cheated on you when you were pregnant. Then you lived with Granny till Jeff "rescued" you. Not really being on your own, is it?

My imaginary argument has got me all wound up, and I'm walking around my room in circles. I try to banish imaginary Mom from my head just as there's a real knock at my door.

"It's Jeff. Can I come in?"

"Um...yeah."

He enters the room as if he's pretending to walk on eggshells, making a big deal of closing the door gently. Sometimes everything about him irritates me. He's got his eyebrows raised and a serious expression on—probably the one he uses when he tells the kids at his school they're going to fail the history final.

"Look, Mia. It's not okay, this snapping at your mom."

"I'll say sorry."

"It's getting to be a pattern with you. Staying at that place night after night. When we do see you, you can't get away fast enough. There's clearly some drinking going on as well."

"You don't know—" I stop myself. "My shifts finish late. Jesus, I thought you'd be glad I'm working hard."

"I am. But you're obviously not sleeping."

I study his face and suddenly feel as though what I *am* doing is written all over my face. He's waiting. Expecting me to confess it all and say he's right and that I'll stop working so much and thank him for caring about me.

"Gabi's been calling the house phone for you," he continues softly. "She said to tell you to 'look at your damn phone.'" He smiles. "From what I can see, you're glued to the thing. What's going on?"

At that moment my phones buzzes in my hand. Jamie. I tilt the screen away so Jeff won't see.

"Can you let it go just once?" he says.

I look up at him, but at the same time open the message. My eyes flick down to read it.

Early swim, Joseph? Hurry up. Being naked on my own is no fun.

My face flushes red. I know he's kidding. He wouldn't be wandering around naked at this time. Guests might see. But is he suggesting...

Jeff reaches out to take my phone and I swerve out of his way. All my anger and annoyance starts to spill over, and I just want to grab him and shake him.

"Oh my God! Can you just get your nose out of my life?"

It's not quite how I meant it to come out, and he looks suitably taken aback, but I can't stop myself.

"Just because you've got no friends, it doesn't mean you can take a creepy interest in *my* social life. It's WEIRD!"

"It's called bringing you up, Mia," he says steadily. "I've been doing it since you were five, and I'm going to keep caring about you whether you like it or not."

"Well, you keep doing that. Just as long as you know you'll always be a terrible replacement for my dad."

He bites the inside of his cheeks. Jeff makes a point of never saying anything bad about Dad. Sometimes I think he does it just so we know how easily he could insult Dad if he wanted to. Dad cheated. Walked out on us. Never visits. Jeff's got a lot of ammunition. The hot anger has been replaced by a cold feeling. I want to hurt him.

"What do you want to say? You're obviously thinking tons of nasty things about Dad, so just say them. What is it? He left us? Well, every day I wish he hadn't, because if my mom hadn't been single and desperate, there's no way she would have ended up with a sad frigging loser like you."

Jeff's staring at me, stunned. He breathes in and I think I'm about to get totally reamed out, but then he just sighs and looks up at the wall. His face is pink and his eyes are blinking rapidly, magnified by his glasses. He turns and walks out of my room.

I'm shaking. I've been pretty horrible to Jeff before, but I've never said anything like that. I sit down and fiddle with my hair and try to shut out the whole thing—along with thoughts of Gabi and my friends and Dan. I'm still friends with them, aren't I? It's not like I've done anything to them. They just don't know what I do at night.

Oh my God, I sound like a vampire.

I pick up my phone.

`Can you pick me up? Probably put some clothes on or you'll get arrested.`

When I tell Mom I'm staying at Gabi's, she looks really pleased. Jeff hasn't told her about our fight yet, so I need to leave quickly. As I'm heading up the driveway, I can only hope that she waits for me to come back to yell at me and doesn't call Gabi's house when I don't answer my cell phone.

I get to the end of my road and see the silver car.

A sort of release breaks over me. I don't know what it is that's driving me to keep going back. I feel like I'm chasing something, some mysterious sensation that I can't even put into words—but I know it's the exact opposite of daily life. Of routine. Of knowing that every day of summer that goes by is another step closer to school and everything that's familiar.

Chapter 24

I sit down. I'm laughing so much I can't breathe. Dan, Gabi, Max, and I are in front of the monkey enclosure. We were doing voice-overs of the monkeys, and Max's one kept getting screwed by the other ones. His outraged face is hilarious. Gabi is practically on the ground. She also has the loudest laugh known to man.

"I'm going to WET MYSELF!" shrieks Gabi.

"I'm actually crying!" Dan says.

"It's not that funny!" Max protests, but he can't help laughing.

"Owww." I lean back and wait for the pain in my ribs to subside.

"What can you do in this situation?" says Dan. "Doughnuts. Doughnuts?"

There's a resounding yes from the three of us, and Dan heads off toward the concession stands.

Gabi grabs my arm, recovering fast. "Omigod. Mia. When you went to the bathroom earlier, Dan totally said he was falling for you!"

I look over at Max, who nods in agreement. "Yup. Loves you, girl."

Gabi looks at me expectantly.

I look over at the back of Dan's head as he waits in the line. And I remember my hands running over it when we kissed. I feel the warm buzz that I get every time I arrive at work and Dan's already in the kitchen.

"His hair looks good, doesn't it?" I say. "Everyone at work's making fun of him for it and calling him Tintin, but I really like it."

"Yeah, um, okay. Mi, I asked if you're falling for him, not if you like his hair."

"Yeah, I know."

"So?"

"Of course I like him. It's just complicated."

"Why?"

I don't answer.

Gabi gives me a look. "Come on."

I eye her warily, as I've got an idea what's coming. She makes a lunge for my head.

"Come to my bosom."

Ever since Year Nine when Gabi was delighted to discover she was growing absolutely enormous boobs, she's always taken the opportunity to rub them in our faces. Literally.

I struggle for a moment, but then let it happen. She clutches my head to her chest, and my face is buried in boob. It's what she does when she wants me to tell the truth. I breathe in, risking intoxication by Ralph Lauren.

130

The situation is so familiar, it makes me feel like everything is normal. Although that might not be the impression that other zoo-goers walking past our bench might get. This is Gabs. I've known her forever. She's the last person I should be keeping secrets from.

"Oay mri aigh ann."

She releases her grip slightly so that I can actually speak.

"Okay, I like Dan."

"Super," says Dan, appearing behind us. "Doughnut?"

Gabi lets me go immediately and I sit up. When Dan's handing out the doughnuts, our eyes meet, and he smiles his lopsided smile. My heart leaps.

Gabi's reading a message on her phone "We're going to meet the others after this," she says. "There's some band with someone's brother in it or something playing. You guys should come."

"What kind of music is it?" Dan says.

"Guitars," says Gabi vaguely while texting. It's safe to say that with gigs, she's more interested in the social side than the music.

"Oh, but Mia's got a family dinner, haven't you?" Dan says.

That gets her attention. She usually gets invited to my family dinners. Not to this one though, obviously, since I made it up.

I'm still feeling the aftermath of the heart-leap moment. "I'll make some excuse," I say.

"Nice!" yells Gabi, and Dan grins at me again. Even Max nods and says, "Sweet."

They are so uncomplicatedly happy to have me around. I feel really bad about how little effort I've put into seeing them this summer.

131

Gabi gets into organizing mode. "So, we'll go back to my house and get ready. Then get some food in town, and we'll be there by eight. Mia, didn't you want to dye your hair? I'll do it for you at my place. We can go to the drugstore on the way home."

"Okay, but no bird poo streaks."

"We do *not* speak of that," she says, and we both crack up. Max and Dan look confused.

"Before either of your times," I explain.

As we leave, I link arms with Gabi. "Can you dye it red?"

Chapter 25

I'm on the late shift, and it's another quiet one. Suzy, Ben-the-other-kitchen-boy, and I sit and chat for most of the night and try to throw peanuts into each other's mouths.

Jamie comes to the bar with his hair even messier than usual and wearing jogging shorts and a T-shirt. He's obviously only just gotten up.

"You look dead," Suzy says. "What were you doing last night?"

Jamie gives a big fake smile. "Now, that would be telling."

"What do you want?" I say quickly.

"Wine, please," says Jamie.

"Make that two."

Everyone looks up at the door. Cleo's back.

She's wearing a tight checked shirt and shorts and has her hair piled on top of her head. She must have come straight from the airport, but she still manages to look effortlessly stunning.

"In fact," she says, waving away the bottle that Suzy's about to open, "save it. We'll all have a drink at the end of your shift. Gives me a chance to make myself up. And you, Jay."

Suzy and Ben-the-other-kitchen-boy say they'll stay for one.

"Joseph?" says Jamie.

"Yeah, count me in," I say.

Cleo looks up. "Oh my God! I didn't recognize you. You've dyed your hair red."

"Yeah!" I say, probably too excitedly.

"It looks great," she says. She's fiddling with her necklace. The pearl drop necklace. "Well, then. A shower, a shit, and a shave." She starts for the door, but Jamie calls after her.

"Joseph and I will go for a swim first."

Surprise flickers across her face, but other than that she doesn't react. "Don't be long."

"It would be easy," he says and disappears under the water. I wait for him to surface again.

I'm standing with my back against the side of the pool with my arms wrapped around myself. Usually I'd be swimming or splashing Jamie, starting up conversations to see where they would go, but tonight is different. I'm thinking about Cleo. Did he know she was coming over? Does he care? I think guiltily that in the last two weeks, it's been pretty easy to forget about her. I peer over at the shape of the castle in the distance. She could be watching from a window. How much could she see from there?

"What do you mean?" I say when he comes up at the other end of the pool. He fixes me with a glance and then goes under again, swimming toward me this time. He rises out of the water about a yard away and looks at me steadily.

"I wouldn't even have to touch you," he says slowly.

The edges of his words make me shiver, although I try to pretend it's the cold. All the questions I wanted to ask him dissolve. I want to know what happens next.

He moves closer and I feel the water lap against me, and just that slight change sends tingles all down me.

"Put your arms down."

I move my arms down by my sides. He puts his hands on the pool edge on either side of me, so he's right up close in front of me. His eyes glide down over my body, and just the way he looks at me makes me breathe quicker. He moves his head toward my shoulder, and then I feel his teeth as he moves my bikini strap to the side.

"Okay," he says, "maybe touch you a little." He pauses. "And a bit more." He bites my bare shoulder gently. And then moves upward and bites my earlobe. I can feel him so close to me in the water, but not quite touching. I want to feel the full weight of him against me.

With his lips right by my ear, he says, "And more?"

I feel like my legs are going to give way, and I can't stop the words coming out, finally admitting out loud that I want it to happen.

"Okay."

"Jamie!" It's Cleo's voice, coming from the grounds. He moves back and sinks down into the water. "We're coming, darling!" he replies, looking at me with his amused grin. He raises his eyebrows at me. "Okay?" he repeats.

I just look at him. My heart is beating a million times a minute, but not from panic—from a strange pulsing excitement that we could have been caught.

"We'd better go," I say.

135

up at Jamie. He's also looking at Cleo. His foot moves slowly up along my calf. I turn to Cleo again but don't move my legs. I start to tell them about the various awful people we encountered at Dezzie's birthday. His foot moves farther, exerting a light pressure, which is tantalizing. I struggle to keep my voice even as I feel the pressure on the inside of my thigh and higher.

And then he stops. I swallow at a break in my story and look at him. His eyes flicker over to me for only a second.

I've trailed off, and everyone must think I've finished my story. Suzy announces that she has to go. Ben, who is possibly a little in love with her, announces that he does too and they can walk out to the parking lot together.

"Oh, good...," says Suzy. She says good-bye and then starts walking back toward reception at a brisk pace. Ben scrambles after her. So it's just the three of us. I use the opportunity to go to the bathroom.

I'm just about to leave the stall when I hear someone else come in. I pause for a moment. I know it's Cleo. She doesn't go into a stall, but stands waiting outside mine. I take a breath and open the door. She stands there with her arms by her sides and watches me while I wash my hands. I walk up to her, and to try to break the tension, I say, "You okay?" and at that moment she grabs my shoulders and pushes me up against the wall.

She lets go but stands right up close to me. Since she's taller, my eyes are about level with her lips. But when I look up into her face, I get a shock.

She looks worried.

"You know what I asked you to do?"

I nod.

"So...What happened?"

"Nothing. I mean, he didn't sleep with anyone or anything. That I know of."

"No one?"

I shake my head.

Cleo looks around and then bites down on her thumbnail. "I thought you'd be...I mean, isn't that a good thing?"

She laughs emptily, still gazing off to the side of me. "It's not the ones he sleeps with that I need to worry about."

I feel my stomach lurch. Like her words are digging hooks into me and dragging me out of this dark room I've made for myself, where I don't have to face anyone or acknowledge what I'm doing. I clench my hands into fists.

Cleo turns back to me. She twirls a strand of my hair in her fingers. "It suits you," she says. I'm looking down at her chest rising and falling.

"Mia, please don't—" She swallows. The room is charged. Something real has opened up between us, and I fight to shut it down. I don't reply.

Suddenly she moves her hand back and drops the strand of hair. Her expression has returned to its usual unaffected, bored look.

"Come on," she says, and we leave.

Jamie is still in his seat when we get back. He has his head thrown back and is staring at the ceiling.

"Jesus, you've been in there for about a year."

"Mia had a bit of"—Cleo gestures to her stomach—"tummy trouble," she mock-whispers.

"What? No, I—"

"I'll meet you in the pool house, Jay."

As she goes, I'm left facing him. His eyebrows are raised

and he looks mildly amused at my outrage. "Where will you be?"

I could bow out now. Get a taxi home. Tell Mom and Jeff I decided not to stay at Gabi's after all. Leave Jamie and Cleo to their twisted relationship and just have my normal daytime life. He twists his mouth to the side and frowns at me. I think of his lips on my skin. Of lying on the grass. Of Cleo's face when she said, "Please don't."

"I'll be in the shower."

Chapter 27

After weeks of using the shower in the well-heated pool house, the cold stone floor of the servants' quarters is a shock. I'm shivering in the rogue guest towel I found as I push the door closed.

I don't lock it.

Hot water runs over me. But instead of feeling alive, I'm starting to feel numb. Have I just made a complete fool of myself? Why am I getting involved? I can't even understand why I'm doing things at the moment or why words come out of my mouth. It just happens.

I wanted to know what he would do.

Then I hear the door open.

I don't look around. There's a gap between the shower curtain and the wall. He can see me. I stand there, and the thought that I'm letting him look at me starts a burning through my body. I run my fingers through my hair and turn to the side.

"Got a towel?"

He laughs. "Of course."

He takes the white towel from the side and holds it up.

"Don't look," I order him.

He obediently bows his head behind the towel, and I step out of the shower and take it from him. As it passes between us, he looks up for a moment. His eyes run over my breasts and hips, and I hear an intake of breath as I wrap the towel around myself.

We stand there for a moment, and then he puts his hand on the back of my neck and pulls me to him. Our lips are almost touching, but not quite. "I want to take you somewhere."

"Okay."

"Okay," he replies, the corners of his mouth curling into a smile.

He takes my hand and leads me back out into the corridor. We run, me still holding my towel around myself, looking around us constantly for any sign of people. My heart is beating a million times a minute, and I can't decide whether I'm thrilled or terrified. Then we reach a door. One of the old wooden ones, like the one I saw on my interview day. As the door opens, I glimpse wooden paneling. Once we're inside, Jamie closes the door and we're plunged into blackness. There's only the sound of our breathing.

The silence and the darkness make me nervous. "Where are we?"

He steps closer. "There are secret passageways all over. They started out as escape routes for priests." He moves my hair away from my shoulder. I can feel his breath on my neck. "But the fifth duke was a randy fellow and used them to get servant girls into his room."

We both start laughing, and he takes my hand, leading me away from the door. I have my other hand keeping my towel on me, so have to trust he won't walk me into anything.

It feels like the passage runs alongside the corridor to the servants' quarters, but the darkness is so disorienting that I could be going in any direction. After a few minutes, he stops. Still holding my hand, he moves it upward and I touch cool metal. I feel around and realize it's the curved banister of a spiral staircase.

"It leads to the master bedroom," he says.

Then his hand is on my other hand, the one holding the towel. He gently moves it upward and the towel slips down. Both my hands are gripping the banister rungs. My skin is on fire, and I just want him to touch me. As he starts kissing my shoulder, a small cry escapes from my lips. His fingers are running over my back and down my legs. He kisses the top of my chest and then runs his mouth down between my breasts and over my stomach and down. The fire running through me has a pulsing center between my legs, and I ache to feel him there.

But just as he gets there, he stops.

"Imagine I'm kissing you there," he says. He kisses me softly at the top of my thigh. And then more firmly on the other side. And then on the inside of my thigh. I feel the tip of his tongue and the graze of his teeth and sometimes only the brush of his lips. Everywhere around, but never there.

There's a tingling feeling building in me and I'm breathing quickly. Then his lips are moving upward again, and his fingers travel up the inside of my leg, higher and higher. The tingling throbs between my legs. The pressure of his hand on my thigh switches to the lightest of touches just as he reaches—

143

I shake and for a second see colors pass in front of my eyes. I cry out as a sweet explosion spreads from between my legs throughout my body, and as I do his mouth finds mine. I push my lips against his fiercely as waves of tingling break over me and he clutches me to him, absorbing every last movement.

And then we're pressed together, listening to each other's breathing, and the fire I was feeling subsides into a warm glow.

"So...," I say and feel him laugh.

He pulls his head back. "How are you doing, Joseph?"

"I'm...increasingly aware that I'm naked."

He steps back from me, and a few seconds later I feel the towel being wrapped around me. I sink forward into his chest, and he squeezes his arms around me and breathes in. Then he kisses me once on the forehead, but leaves his lips there for a while.

"I suppose we should sleep," he says. "Will the master bedroom do?"

"Don't your parents sleep there?"

"Yes. Is that a problem?"

"You're, like, kiddng, right?"

"Yes, I 'like' am." He grabs my hand again. "They figured out that they can rake in even more cash by letting guests stay there. But it's empty tonight."

The spiral staircase leads to a room that must be tiny, because I can stretch out my arm and touch the wall on either side and can feel the ceiling not too far above my head. Jamie goes ahead of me, and I hear steps creaking and the sound of him loosening something. There's a cracking sound, and then rays of blue light suddenly break through. He's opening a trap door.

The four-poster bed is enormous. I slide my legs around on the duvet as Jamie goes back down to the showers to get my stuff. He leaves me his T-shirt to wear.

There's a huge window covering most of the opposite wall, so the room is flooded with moonlight. It looks out over the grounds at the back of the castle. If I went and looked out, I would be able to see the pool house. Where Cleo is waiting. I shift on the duvet again, more uncomfortably this time. What happens now?

I'm interrupted by the trap door opening and Jamie lobbing my bag into the room.

"Watch out! You'll break my... clothes," I say.

He lifts himself up into the room and doesn't acknowledge my comment. He's wearing only his jeans, and the moonlight bounces off his muscled chest. I get a flashback to the passageway, and an echo of what I felt ripples through me.

Then he stands at the end of the bed and drops his jeans.

Slightly in shock, I say the first thing that comes into my head. "Easy, tiger."

He completely cracks up. I start laughing too and struggle to get my words out. "That... was ridiculous, though. What... What are you doing?"

"Sleeping. Are you going to take up the whole bed, tiger?"

We both slide under the covers and lie there, looking up at the ceiling.

The question forms in my head, but I can't say it out loud. What happens tomorrow?

"Oh my God, tomorrow!" I make him jump.

"What?" he says.

"It's when we get our exam grades."

"I don't suppose you have anything to worry about."

"No...Well, I don't know. I need five Bs to stay on track for university. It's just...I'd hoped to...do something else. Like, travel or something. It feels like from tomorrow, everything's set."

He doesn't reply. I realize I don't even know what he's doing next year.

"What about you?" I ask, turning to face him.

He stays on his back, looking upward. "Nothing." He frowns.

"Didn't you get in—"

"I didn't apply. My parents don't know yet. They think I'm off to Durham."

"How?"

"I faked some letters," he says, like that's not a big deal.

He turns onto his side, facing me. "Mom will have a stroke when she finds out. Dad will brush it off with some comment about how you don't need a degree to succeed in the city. I'll reveal I'm not doing that either, and he can have his stroke then."

The mention of his dad sends a wave of bitterness across his face. And then he leans forward and kisses me on the lips. For a moment, I feel what I do around Dan. Warmth, easiness, and something real.

"'Night," he says.

"'Night," I reply, but we keep facing each other, eyes open.

We talk for hours, to the point where we can't keep our eyes open and what we're saying starts to not make sense. Silence falls, and I give into the tiredness.

It's a light sleep, though, because with a creak of the bed my eyes snap open again. I'm facing away from Jamie. The mattress moves as he slides off. I don't give any sign that

146

I'm awake. I lie there listening to him pulling his jeans back on and opening the trap door quietly and carefully, then shutting it with only a small thud.

Mentally plotting out his route, I slide out of the bed and go to the window. I have it exactly right. He comes out from underneath the window, where the archways are, and heads onto the path to the pool house.

The warm feeling in my chest slowly disintegrates.

I wonder if he'll turn and look at the window, but he keeps walking, hands thrust into his pockets. A few moments after he enters the pool house, the lights come on.

Chapter 28

I barely sleep. I'm mostly just staring up at the ceiling and rerunning the night's events. Alone in this big room, I'm struggling to remember how I could have felt so confident. The sheets are startlingly white and clinical. And cold.

When the sky starts to brighten, I get up and look out the window again. There's mist hanging over the grounds, and the whole landscape looks still.

I decide I'll sneak out now and walk to Gabi's. Her mom's taking us in to get our grades. I'm not even sure what time it is, but I can find a bench to sit on or something if it's too early for her to be up.

I take off Jamie's T-shirt and lift my bag up onto the bed. I've taken to bringing extra clothes with me after all these nights staying out, so I have a normal dress and leggings to wear. I keep looking through the bag for my phone to find out the time, but I can't find it. Damn. I must have left it behind the bar.

I try to make the room look unused and pray that the cleaners get to it before Julia does. I go to the trap door and pull on the iron ring to heave it open. Going down the steps, I stumble briefly and let go of the door. It shuts with a crash above me. I feel my way through the tiny room and onto the staircase, along the wall, and stop at the first door I come to. I'll just have to hope it's the right one.

I want to punch the air as I come out into the servants' quarters. I slip out, shut the door, and walk straight into a cleaner. She frowns at me.

"Good morning," I say and bow my head, which I don't think she finds particularly normal. I hurry away before she decides to alert someone.

Now to retrieve my phone from the bar and leave. I'm beginning to think that it's actually pretty fun, this sneaking around—I'm playing the James Bond theme in my head, and...Oh, crap. It's Dan.

I do what no sane person would do and dive under a table. I watch Dan's feet go past as he walks through the restaurant to the kitchen. I plot out a sprint to the bar and then the quickest route to the door.

"Dan!" Julia's feet appear at the restaurant entrance. And now more feet. She calls him back over and explains that these guests have to get a flight and so have asked for an early breakfast.

Soon Dan's leading them over to a table. My table. Of course. There's the creak of a seat as some pinstriped legs and shiny black shoes appear on my right, then a more delicate creak as tights and slightly too small slip-on heels appear to my left. I literally have no idea what to do.

"Tea or coffee?" says Dan.

"Coffee, please," says a nasal male voice.

I really need to tell someone I'm here.

It's decided for me when, as the woman asks for tea, she nudges the slip-on shoes off her feet, stretches out her leg, and kicks me. There's a shriek, and then a heavily made-up fifty-something face appears beside me.

"Hello! I'm just cleaning under this table." I start rubbing the floor. With my hands. Then Dan's face appears.

"Hi, Dan. I'm just…cleaning."

"I think it's clean now," he says. I can't decide whether he's looking at me with fear or pity.

I crawl out, dragging my bag after me, and stand up. "Good, well, that's clean. Tea or coffee?"

"We've ordered," says the man, who looks a little like a weasel in a suit.

Dan escorts me to the bar, where he starts making the tea and coffee. He makes an extra cup of tea and plunks it in front of me before he goes back to the couple. While he's gone, I grab my phone and stuff it into my bag.

He walks back over. "What…? Why?"

"I finished late last night—there was this table that stayed forever. So I slept here."

"Under a table?"

"No! In the servants' quarters."

Unsurprisingly, he's still interested to know why he found me hiding under a table, cleaning the floor with my hands. I come up with some ridiculous explanation that I thought he was Julia. Although that doesn't explain anything, he seems to accept it, which makes me slightly concerned about his level of intelligence. But then, I suppose, why would he think I would lie?

Chapter 29

"Ha! What are you doing, you freak?"

I was sitting on the low brick wall outside Gabi's house and must have fallen asleep. I had my head on my knees, so I probably did look a little weird.

Then Gabi's mom comes barreling past me, chattering away on her phone, and doesn't even notice me. I follow them to the car.

At school, Gabi manages to persuade her mom to wait in the car rather than accompany us for the actual grades part.

"Oh, go on. That's right. You girls have your moment!" She squeezes my hand and grins at me.

Gabi's already started toward the entrance, and I run to catch up with her.

"You look dead," she says.

"Oh, thanks, Gabs."

We find the rest of the gang and have a huge group hug. A

few people say how they haven't seen me in forever, but soon we slip into normal conversations and gossip and we collect our envelopes. We're all opening them together. We count to three.

There's a flurry of screaming and waving papers around. Lots of As and A-pluses are flying back and forth. Most of us got a C in media, but to be fair, we spent the majority of those classes making videos of the adventures of a little LEGO man we found. I skim mine. Mostly Bs. A couple of As. An A-plus in food tech, which is an absolute joke.

I don't really feel anything. I know I've passed everything, but my mind's still running through how I can get out.

We're interrupted by a man with a camera who seems to be looking for blond people he can take pictures of opening their results and jumping in the air. He says he's from the local newspaper, which hopefully is true and he's not just a pervert. That's when I realize that Gabi hasn't said anything. She's just staring at her grades.

I stand next to her.

"I didn't pass," she says quietly. "I didn't get five Bs. I got a..." Her voice wobbles, and she swallows. "I got a D in math."

She looks around at all the whooping and excited chatter. "I thought I'd...I'd made it up."

She has her head down and her shoulder bowed. I've never seen her looking this crushed. It is sort of taken for granted that everyone at our school will pass their exams and then stay on for the next two years to do A-Levels. There's a community college where you can do your A-Levels, but if we all stay at school she'll be going on her own.

"They might let you in," I say. "Or you can go to the

community college. Or do something else. I was thinking of—"

She interrupts me. "You've got the option, though."

We're silent for a while. I squeeze her hand, and she puts her head on my shoulder. I feel hot tears soaking into my dress.

"I don't want to go to the party anymore," she says, her voice tight. "Can we do something? Just you, me, Max, and Dan?"

"Yeah," I say. "Of course."

She lifts her head. "Oh, I know, we should have a meal! At your work. Don't you get a really good discount? And WINE."

A weight drops in my stomach. She looks at me expectantly, her eyes still wet with tears.

"Yep, sure." I nod.

"Call them now!" she says.

With every ring I'm willing Dan not to answer. I wanted to get away from that place for a night. I don't even know how I'm supposed to act around Jamie. Or Cleo.

"Good morning, Radleigh Castle Restaurant. Dan speaking. How may I help?"

Oh, good.

Chapter 30

"What's foy grass? Anyway, I'll have a bottle of the sove."

Gabi addresses the first question to no one in particular, but her drink order to Melanie, who is our waitress.

"One bottle of the Soave," says Melanie sweetly, making a point of saying "Soave" in an Italian accent. "How many glasses?"

"Just a straw," says Gabi. Then she sees Melanie's shocked expression. "Kidding! Two. For me and Mi. Ha! That's me and her, not myself twice."

Since we got the grades, Gabi's gone into overdrive.

Dan orders a beer, and Max asks for a glass of Rioja.

We all look at him in shock.

"What?" he says. "My mom gives it to me with meals."

We suppress our laughter at Max as Melanie arches an eyebrow and writes down our order. Dan's eighteen, so technically we're accompanied by an adult, and we are eating, but it still feels a little sketchy ordering alcohol. I wish we'd gotten a different waitress.

I'm sure I hear her give a world-weary sigh as she struts back off to the kitchen.

When the first course arrives, Gabi proposes a toast. "GCSEs can suck it!" She cheers and we all clink glasses. I see a few guests turn around and look at us, but thankfully Julia isn't around. The instant I think that, she walks into the room. Following her are a large woman with cropped blond hair and an upturned nose and an equally large girl with long blond hair and a similarly upturned nose, who must be her daughter. They stand in the corner while Julia and the older woman point at different places in the room and the girl fiddles with a notepad.

They drift past us, still talking.

"But we can't have the food table there; it will be too near the DJ," squawks the large woman, putting the emphasis on the "J" of "DJ."

"Don't have a DJ," says Gabi through a mouthful of bread.

"I'm sorry?" says the woman.

Julia's eyes flash dangerously, and I kick Gabi under the table, but she ignores me.

"Don't have a DJ," she says. "It's so gauche. He'll play eighties' crap that no one young has heard of. Rent a jukebox and let the guests pick the music they want to hear."

The girl's eyes light up and she whispers, "Oh, Mom, I'd like a jukebox."

"Yeah, *and* then you'll have more money for champagne." Gabi smiles.

"It does sound 'trendy,' doesn't it?" says the mom, doing a little jig. "Write it down, Mary."

Her daughter grins excitedly and scribbles on the pad.

"Thank you!" says the mom and waddles off to do more organizing.

Julia turns to the table. "Yes, thank you...?"

"Gabi," says Gabi.

Julia nods. "And are you enjoying your dinner, Gabi?"

"Yeah," says Gabi, "although you should have a dinner deal. I'd be paying out of my ass for this if we didn't have Mia's discount."

"Noted," says Julia, her face unreadable.

"And the shrimp is small. Omigod, Mia, do you remember when I thought that was all shrimp was and I didn't know they'd had the heads and legs taken off and I was all, 'But where's its *brain*?'" She turns to Julia. "It was so funny."

Julia smiles her serial-killer smile.

"So we'll call you if we want anything, right?" says Gabi, and I widen my eyes in shock.

But Julia just nods. "Of course," she says and walks away.

Gabi looks at my face. "What?" she says. Then light dawns. "Oh my God, is that the one who's a total bitch?"

Julia, who is only a few yards away, pauses for a split second and then continues walking.

I finish off my glass of wine in one gulp.

Chapter 31

After the meal, we walk out onto the terrace. Ever so slightly tipsy, Gabi clings to me.

"It's frigging beautiful here." She sighs. "You guys are lucky."

Dan and I look at each other. "Yeah, we are, I suppose," he says.

"Good evening," says a voice, and my heart stops.

"I understand you're celebrating," continues Jamie's cool voice.

"Drowning our sorrows," says Gabi. "I messed up my exams," she adds confidentially.

"Well, we're having a little party down there." He nods toward the pool house. "You'd all be very welcome. I'm Jamie, by the way."

"Gabi. We've met." Gabi goes forward and kisses him on both cheeks. Max goes to fist-bump him, and Jamie just looks at him curiously. He turns to me.

"Do I get a kiss from you too?"

I stand on tiptoe and awkwardly align my cheek with his, aiming just to bump them together, but he moves around and the kiss gets the side of my mouth. I glare at him as he greets Dan, standing behind me.

"Hello, Kitchen Dan."

Dan just nods.

Jamie points toward the pool house. "Shall we? We're just about to pass the port."

I had an insane, delusional hope that Gabi might say she's tired and it's high time we went home, but she's already hobbling down the path in her heels, yelling, "Save some for me!"

Max shrugs and says, "What my lady wants..." and then follows her.

Jamie looks at us questioningly.

Dan puts his arm around me. "Yeah, we'll be along in a minute," he says. I feel a twinge of annoyance at him.

Jamie widens his eyes. "Play safe." And then he's gone.

I step away from Dan's arm.

"Hey, Mia, can I talk to you?"

I turn to face him but don't want to look him in the eye. Instead, it now looks like I'm very interested in his sleeve.

"Mia?"

"Yeah."

"Are you okay?"

"Yeah, fine."

"You've been a little quiet."

"Oh, no, I'm just tired."

"Okay. I was worried. This morning I found you hiding under a table. I just wanted to make sure everything was all right."

I can feel my resolve wobbling. I was going to tell him we

158

should just be friends. But as I look in his eyes, the words are slipping farther and farther away.

"It's just…I don't think…"

He looks at me, his eyebrows raised in genuine concern. Everything about Dan is genuine. And warm. And caring.

"Don't put your arm around me just because there's some other guy around. It's like you're saying I'm yours or something."

Dan nods gravely. "Like I'm pissing on you."

It completely breaks the tension, and we dissolve into laughter.

"Yes, just like that."

He nods. "Sorry. I know it was a little dickish. That guy just gets to me a bit. He's pretty full of himself."

I consider all the things I could say. *You've got nothing to worry about. You're ten times better than him.* Instead I say, "If it makes you feel any better, he's pretending he got into college."

As soon as it's out of my mouth, I want to reel it back in. This is one of those moments—and I have many of them—when I wish there was an undo button in real life.

"Seriously? Why the hell's he doing that? Ha! That does make me feel better, actually."

Shit. Shit. Shit. "Don't say anything, though." There's a desperate tinge to my voice.

"No, 'course not."

And my thumping heart slows a little.

"Mia, there was something else I wanted to say."

We walk into the pool house a few minutes later, holding hands. And the first person we see is Cleo. I meet her eyes, and guilt thumps through me. She takes note of the handholding and looks like she's carefully selecting her words. There's a glint of danger in her eyes.

"Your friend's fun," she says eventually, gesturing behind her. Gabi is up on a table, leading a vigorous dance to Rihanna. Behind her, an enthusiastic Max appears to be teaching people how to rap.

"Yeah, she is," I say, feeling fiercely proud. This is Gabi's night, and I don't want my dramas to ruin it. I walk around the table and Gabi grabs my hands. We dance to the end of the song with her still on the table and me on the floor. The next song is one Gabi doesn't like, so she announces that she's going for a pee. Dan's gone to see if he can find any drinks, and so I sit down next to Max on the sofa.

"You guys like the drama, don't you?" I say to him.

"Yeah, man," he replies. "Messes with my head sometimes, but I couldn't be without it, you know what I mean?"

"So it's worth it? All the fighting and stuff?"

"Yeah, 'course," he tells me. "We argue, like, every week, but I'd never go near anyone else. I totally love that girl."

It's the sweetest thing I've ever heard Max say. And then he ruins it by adding, "You get me?"

I sigh. There've been times when I've been mean about Gabi and Max and their shouting matches and passionate public making-up sessions. But at least it's honest. This morning I was going to cool things off with Dan, and now, following our talk on the terrace, I think we might be "officially going out." If I could just stick with that, I'd be happy. I look over at Jamie. Happy, instead of scared, nervous, uncertain...excited.

There's a slight commotion at the door. Melanie walks in, Simon shuffling in her wake. She waves at us.

"Thought we'd come and see what all the fuss is about!" She turns to Simon. "See, Si, it would be perfect for the reception."

I don't know if it has occurred to her that Jamie lives here and might not let his house be invaded for a wedding.

A whoop comes from the other side of the room. We both turn to see Gabi heading back from the bathroom. As if to illustrate Max's point, she gets called over by Jamie's friend Guy, and when he attempts to grope her, she slaps him. She runs back over and vaults into Max's lap.

Dan appears a minute later, drinkless, which is probably a good thing. We've now taken over the sofa. The sofa I've slept on. Gabi lies across us.

"I LOVE you guys," she says. "Can I sleep here?"

In unison we reply "No" and roll her off. And then the music stops as a bored voice rings through the pool house.

"I'd like to play a little game."

Chapter 32

"It's lovely to see you here, Melanie," says Jamie. "And Simon."

Melanie looks a little surprised to be singled out. Simon looks terrified.

"Wedding plans going well?"

"Oh, fantastic," says Melanie, and then rambles on about how they're looking into having it at Radleigh, because it's classic, you know? Jamie yawns, but it doesn't deter her. Then I notice Simon. He's shaking his head. And then he mouths, "Please." At Jamie.

"That's wonderful, really. I'm not surprised, because Simon has been sending me some very enthusiastic texts."

Melanie's cheeriness falters slightly. "Really?"

"Really." Jamie smiles innocently. "Although, I have to say I found them rather confusing. Is it *your* 'magnificent penis' he wants me to send a picture of? I wasn't aware you had one."

Melanie and Simon don't say anything. Jamie reads out Simon's messages to the amusement of some of the room, particularly Guy. Some of the words make Melanie turn and look at Simon. They clearly sound like things Simon would say. Some people look shocked. Cleo, sitting with Nish and Effy, looks bored.

Simon looks heartbroken. I wonder what Jamie said to him that day Simon marched off to confront him. It must have started then. He's obviously hooked Simon in and gotten him to let loose these feelings that now seem completely crazy.

Jamie's good at that, I think. And the thought chills me.

Eventually Melanie turns and walks out of the room. Simon pauses for a moment, looks sadly at Jamie, and then follows her.

There's no big shouting match this time. It's clear their relationship is broken.

The four of us on the sofa have been sitting in silence, but then Gabi finds her voice.

"What the hell was that about?" she shrieks.

Dan stands up. "This is messed up." He shakes his head and heads for the door.

Gabi, Max, and I all get up to go with him. We're just getting to the pool when a voice calls out, "Joseph, wait."

Dan and Max are already too far away to hear, but Gabi, who's just ahead of me, stops and turns around too.

"I need to speak to you," Jamie says to me.

"Um...why?" Gabi asks.

"Gabi, it's fine. I...We won't be long."

"Okay...," she says slowly. "I'll go get a taxi and come back for you in a minute, okay?"

As her footsteps fade, Jamie looks at me with his arms crossed.

"Swimming tonight?"

"You must be kidding."

"Someone told me I don't make jokes."

"You just wrecked someone's relationship. For no reason. They weren't some horrible old couple who had it coming. They did nothing to you."

"Because it's all fake," he snaps. "It's classic wedding venues and personalized phone cases and going through the stages—university, jobs, marriage, babies—and none of it's real. We do it because we should."

"But they were happy."

"Are you happy?"

"What? Yes. I'm really happy. Dan's…He's invited me to go to Paris with him at the end of the summer. We're really… going out now."

Jamie's face is unreadable. "I look forward to seeing your phone case."

"Right. So, can I go now?"

Jamie laughs to himself.

"What?"

"I just know, come two o'clock, you'll be here, or in the shower."

"I won't."

"You will, Mia. You love me."

Now it's my turn to laugh. "That's where you're wrong. This…'thing' never had anything to do with love. I was attracted to you. I don't feel anything else. I don't love you. I love Dan."

"Well," says Jamie evenly. "Good for Dan."

He's looking behind me and I turn my head. Dan has just reached the edge of the pool. I don't know how much he heard.

"The taxi's here," he says.

"Enjoy your new girlfriend, pot washer," says Jamie.

Anger flashes across Dan's face. "Well, you enjoy university, okay?"

Jamie freezes, and then his eyes meet mine. We all stand there in silence.

"Well, if we're sharing...," Jamie says slowly. He pulls his phone from his pocket, presses a few buttons, and then shows me the screen.

It's that picture. The one Kieran sent around his entire school.

I feel sick. I chase him back to the pool house but stop at the window. He's showing his phone to people. They're pointing at the screen, slapping him on the back, some craning around to try to see. I'm shaking. It's happened again, and, just like the first time, I'm completely powerless. People are looking at me. Judging me. And I have no control.

My eyes are full of tears and I can't see. I spin around and collide with Dan. His face is a mixture of anger and confusion as he tries to read my expression for clues. He tries to put his arms around me, but I push him away and run. I hear him calling after me as I stumble toward the parking lot and find Gabi. I run into her arms and she hugs me fiercely, even though she doesn't know why.

Chapter 33

Jamie Elliot-Fox is toxic.

I don't write in my diary much. Gabi and I used to write them side by side when we were younger, so there's lots of stuff like *I secretly totally love Kieran Saunders. Don't tell!* and *I luv Max Holmes and his sexy body!* written about fifty times by Gabi.

There's some stuff in there from when I was going out with Kieran, but it's all written like I thought someone was reading over my shoulder. It's all about how we were soul mates and "knew each other inside out." Nothing about feeling uncomfortable, secretly panicking, and sending naked pictures. I kept those parts in my head.

But there's no pretending with Jamie. He's damaged, and I need to tell myself that. Just in case at some point I start to kid myself that he's normal.

"I'm with you there," says Gabi, peering over my shoulder. "What a dickhead."

I take a deep breath. "Gabi?" I've rehearsed the story in my head. It's going to start with, "I've been an idiot."

But she doesn't hear me.

"I don't understand why anyone would go near him. Melanie and Simon and that leggy girl he's going out with all need their heads examined. The girlfriend must either be stupid or just as evil as him."

The words evaporate from my tongue. "Yeah, I know."

"Mrs. Elliot-Fox? I need to cut down on my shifts."

Julia doesn't look up from her desk. "Oh?"

"Yeah, I'm getting tired, and I haven't been getting any A-level reading done and..."

"It's encouraging to hear that A-Levels do at least require reading. Bring me the schedule when you're done."

I take the schedule sheet out and lean it on the bar, crossing out my name in various squares.

"Gin and tonic, please."

"Sorry, I don't actually work on the bar—"

Cleo laughs. "I didn't ask for a chat. I asked for a gin and tonic."

I keep looking down at the schedule sheet. "I don't work on the bar. I'm not eighteen. You know that."

"For fuck's sake, I'll get it myself." She goes behind the bar and grabs the bottle of Tanqueray from the shelf. "You shouldn't go shouting about your age," she says. "I'm pretty sure you're not supposed to get your tits out before you're eighteen either."

There's a nastiness to her voice that I've heard directed at other people but never at me, and it hits me like a slap. A cold realization dawns that I haven't been doing anything to earn her

167

friendship. I don't know what she knows, but I know that the wrong side of Cleo is not a safe place to be.

I grab the schedule sheet and walk quickly to the door, my face burning. I try to compose myself in the corridor outside Julia's office before going back in.

When she looks over the sheet, she arches one of her eyebrows. "All the ones you've kept are those working with Dan," she says.

"I..." But I can't think of anything to say.

"Young love," Julia says dryly. "Is there anything else? Because I have to find people to fill those shifts now."

"No, thank you. That was it."

When I'm nearly at the door, Julia says, "Your friend, the loud one..."

"Gabi?"

"She left this." Julia holds up a customer comment card covered in Gabi's bubbly handwriting. "Lots of pointers for me. Do convey my gratitude."

Jeff's in his study planning lessons when I hover at the door and tell him that I've cut down on my shifts.

"That's good, love," he says, not looking up.

"I brought you some tea."

He turns around. "Oh, come here."

I shuffle over to him, and Jeff hugs me for the first time since I was about seven.

"I'm sorry," I mumble into his cardigan.

"I'm made of strong stuff," he says, giving me a squeeze. "You should hear some of the things my students have said to me. Now, if you want to be picked up from your late shifts, you just have to say so."

I nod.

"Except for Wednesdays. Eric and I are going to trivia night. I thought I'd get myself one of those 'social lives.'"

I grin at him. As I leave, I realize Mom is standing on the stairs outside the study.

She kisses me on the top of my head. "Thank you," she says.

"S'all right." I smile at her and turn to go.

"Ooh, wait," she says, fishing something out of her bag. "I won this in the work summer raffle. Can you believe it? I've entered every year and never gotten more than an assortment of chocolates."

She hands me an envelope, which I open.

"Oh my God!" I say. It's a ticket to Paris.

"So, do you want it? You said you and Dan were planning a trip."

"What? Are you serious? Don't you and Jeff want it?"

"Jeff took me to Paris on our first anniversary. Granny told me you spent the weekend in a rotten mood because we didn't take you. It's only fair!"

I can't wait to tell him. But for a moment, the wrong face flashes before my eyes.

Chapter 34

Dan pokes me with a wooden spoon. "Earth to Mia," he says.

"Sorry. I was daydreaming."

"What about?"

"Nothing. Paris."

I haven't told him about the tickets yet. I need to soon—he's planning his route and might book the hostel or something.

"Huh. Did you know there's a zoo there?"

He's already on his way out the door. I run after him.

"I did not. We'll have to have a monkey day."

Coming out of the reception door, I realize Jamie's sitting on the main steps. I don't know if I even see him, but I feel him there.

I grab Dan's hand, trying to dispel the shameful thought that I'm doing what I yelled at him for. I swing his arm. Like a child, I think too late. Sooner or later he's going to notice that nothing I do is normal.

"We'll do the art and shit, yah?"

He laughs. "Yah, like the Louvre and shit. Totes."

Along the pathway to the park, I think I hear the crunch of feet behind us. I wonder if Jamie has followed us.

The park opens out, and we're at the part where there's a line of trees on each side pointing back toward town. I stop and pull Dan back by his arm. I stand on tiptoe and press my lips onto his. We'd be in full view of the end of the path.

Dan looks down at me with a half smile. With our hands still clasped, he runs his thumb along my knuckles. "What are you looking at?"

I turn back. "Nothing." I focus on his face. I try to imagine a bubble closing around us.

"You know, Paris is just the start," he says. "There'll be Hawaii at the midterm break. Chile at Christmas."

"Eastbourne at Easter when we run out of money."

"I love you a little bit, Mia."

He feels my hand tense and watches me apprehensively. The feeling in my chest is warm, like melting. But there's something deeper. A buzz. The outlines of words, not fully formed. I fight it down and cling to the warmness.

I put my arms around his neck and he stumbles backward, his back making contact with a tree. And I kiss him. Pressing against him and digging my fingers into his skin. I picture the bubble again. Just us.

The buzz continues in the background. I don't allow the words to form, but other things escape occasionally and move in front of my eyes.

Bare legs touching in water.

Pink sky.

Teeth grazing my shoulder.

Chapter 35

I start scraping the food into the garbage can and loading the dishwasher. Dan called in sick today, so I've been half on kitchen duty and half in the restaurant. I'm beginning to regret saying that I would finish cleaning so that Andreas could go. My feet really hurt.

When it's finally clean and I think Jeff is probably already in the parking lot, I come out of the kitchen to get my phone and bag.

Jamie's standing there in the empty restaurant.

"I'd like to talk to you."

The panic that gripped me when I first saw him is gradually transforming into a feeling of white-hot anger.

"Why?" I feel my voice shaking. "Why the HELL would I want to talk to you?"

"I need to explain some things."

I give a hollow laugh. "I really, *really* don't see how you can."

"You don't understand."

"I understand fine, thanks. You betrayed—no. You didn't even betray my trust, because I never trusted you with anything."

His jaw clenches and his eyes narrow angrily. "I trusted you with something."

"You were just boasting. You can lie to anyone. Great. Well done. I hope that makes you happy, because it's all you've got."

He moves closer, our eyes fixed on each other. "I'm not the only one whose relationship is a lie."

I walk forward. My heart is pounding. Everything about the way he's standing there is fueling the burning rage that I can feel pulsing through my hands.

"I hate you."

"I hate what you do to me," he shouts back.

And then his lips are on mine. We're kissing, forcefully, almost hungrily. The anger flowing through every part of me has set me on fire. His hands move over my back, but not in the controlled way they did before—in a frenzied way, like he *needs* to touch me.

We stumble backward and I land against a table. We move together again and I pull him closer, feeling the weight of him on my chest and between my legs. Cutlery is swept off the table and clatters to the ground. The friction of our clothes as he moves against me starts a buzz running through my body. Aching for him is almost painful.

The shrill tone of the restaurant telephone blasts through the room. We stop abruptly and he lifts his head. We slowly sit up, looking at each other and trying to catch our breath.

"Mia…"

"Leave me alone." I slide off the table and walk toward the phone, smoothing down my skirt.

"Good evening, Radleigh Castle Restaurant. Mia speaking. How may I help you?"

"Hi, love, it's Jeff. You weren't answering your phone. I'm outside."

Chapter 36

There are noises coming from the pool house. A dull, angry ache goes through me as I think of them all in there. I clang the plates together as I pick them up off the table. Then I hear some squealing and a splash. I look over at the pool and see a massive white hat moving around with a person under it. It looks like it's Dezzie who's having the party rather than Jamie.

I can't lose the feeling of nervousness. I got asked to change my shift today at the last minute by Julia, so for the second day in a row I'm not working with Dan. There's not much I can do. I can't really tell her that I don't trust myself to be on my own. Especially after yesterday.

So far tonight there's been no sign of him. Or Cleo. I've been willing the hours to go by quickly so I can escape without seeing either of them.

And I feel treacherous that I can't help looking around

for him as I walk through to reception to meet Jeff, but he doesn't appear.

Jeff is sitting there in silence while Andy, who handles the nighttime reception duty, just stares at him. He jumps up when I arrive, and we start out across the gravel to the parking lot.

I can make out the Volvo in the gloom. And a familiar silhouette standing next to it.

I want to scream in frustration. But then I look more closely. I think he's carrying someone.

As we near the car, I see Jeff squinting too. "Who's...? Excuse me? Who are you?"

I'm now close enough to see that Jamie is holding Dezzie. And she's unconscious. He has an expression of pure panic. He looks briefly at Jeff, but speaks to me.

"Please...Can you help? I think she's taken something. I need to get her to a hospital."

"Good Lord," says Jeff. "We should call an ambulance."

"Can we meet it somewhere?" says Jamie. "If my parents find out she's been near drugs, they'll...I can't drive her. I've been drinking." His voice dries up.

"Right. Okay. Right," says Jeff. "Okay. Get in."

I meet Jamie's eye as I walk around the car, but it seems like he's looking right through me.

Jeff revs the engine as Jamie lays Dezzie out on the back seat so that her head is in his lap.

"Oh, I'll just take you there. It will be quicker," mutters Jeff.

"I didn't know who else to ask," says Jamie quietly. He stares at Dezzie the whole way there.

I watch him in the side mirror. He looks terrified. I would

be too, if anything bad happened to Matthew. I wonder if that's what Jeff is thinking. His knuckles have turned white on the steering wheel. I've never seen him drive this fast. Usually he makes a point of going ten miles per hour below the speed limit.

Near the hospital is a whole confusion of one-way streets and ambulance-only routes, so Jamie gets out and starts carrying Dezzie to the entrance while we try to navigate our way to the parking lot.

Jeff goes to pay, and when he leans back into the car to put the ticket in the window, I burst into tears.

"Hey," he says, putting his hand on my shoulder. "She'll be fine. A stomach pump at most, I imagine. She wouldn't be the first."

I nod, but keep on crying. I don't tell him I'm crying about everything. Everything that's happened since I started this job. I'm even crying with shame at the fact that I'm still upset about my selfish little dramas when something real like this is going on.

Jeff stays there, half out of the car with one knee on the seat, rubbing my back for a while. He must be really uncomfortable. Then he goes to see what's going on.

I sit, waiting in the car, barely moving.

Jeff comes back first, saying he couldn't find them. He looks around worriedly, with his hand on the side of the car, but then we see them both walking back through the parking lot.

Dezzie is walking, but she looks shaky and upset. It was just alcohol, apparently, no drugs. Dezzie protests in a small voice that she didn't have very much, and Jeff replies, "For someone of your size, it doesn't need to be very much."

On the drive back to Radleigh, Dezzie sits hugging her knees and looking out the window.

"You can sleep in the pool house. If any of your stupid little friends are still there, I'm kicking them out," says Jamie darkly.

As they're climbing back out of the car, Jamie puts his hand on the back of Jeff's seat. "Thank you, Jeff."

Then he looks over at me. His eyes are shining, all of the usual performance stripped away.

"I hope she's okay," I say quietly.

He nods, and is gone.

An hour later, I'm in bed in my pajamas. Awake.

My phone buzzes.

I'm outside. Can you let me in?

As I'm opening the front door, Jeff appears at the top of the stairs.

"Jamie, you're back," he says groggily.

"Hattie and Harri are keeping a vigil at her bedside." Jamie's voice is croaky. "There wasn't room at the pool house. And I felt…a bit…"

"In need of some tea?" says Jeff.

Five minutes later Jamie is presented with a mug. Jeff says that he can stay over.

"On the sofa," he adds as he goes up the stairs.

I listen to the pad of his slippers as he gets to the bedroom and can't help smiling for a second when I catch Jamie's eye.

Chapter 37

"Can you sit with me while I drink my tea?"

"Um, yeah."

I sit on the edge of the chair opposite the sofa and look past him. Thoughts are whizzing back and forth in my brain faster than I can process them.

"I didn't show the photo of you," he says suddenly.

I look at him then. "I saw you."

He shakes his head. "It was a video. Just some random crap I found. The kind of thing that amuses them."

"Cleo brought it up the next day. I thought it was because you'd shown everyone."

"I did show her," he admits. "On the day I got Kieran to give it to me. She defended you. Said I was a sick, twisted bastard."

"You are," I mutter.

"I've deleted it," he says. "You can check." He slides his

phone across the floor. I don't pick it up. It's easier to hate him.

"I don't know why I'm like this."

I look up at him. His eyes are glistening. He frowns and swallows. "I don't know—" His voice cracks.

I dig my fingernails into my knees. I don't want to look at him. Something I've been keeping hidden is breaking through. Something fierce and powerful. I can feel it humming in my chest, and I want to drown it out.

I keep looking at the floor. I don't know if he's looking at me or not.

"I'm different with you."

I fiddle with my fingers. Eventually I let my eyes move upward and meet his.

"Mia, I'm in love with you."

It's the change in his expression. He looks upset and unsure and scared. I realize that he doesn't know what I'm going to say back. When he was standing outside the pool house and he claimed to know that I loved him, it was all a front. He doesn't know how I feel.

I suppose I haven't really admitted it to myself.

My answer is to move across to the sofa and sit next to him. He turns to look at me, his eyebrows still knitted in uncertainty.

I lean over and kiss him.

We creep into my room. I click the door closed and slide the lock across.

We stand facing each other at the end of my single bed.

I try to steady my breathing. "I haven't ... Well, I have sort of, but I don't really know ..."

"It's okay," he says and kisses me again. The kissing is delicate and tentative this time, every movement of our hands sending ripples of pleasure across my skin as I think of what's about to happen.

He takes off his shirt and shorts and I take off my pajamas, but we collapse into giggles when my foot gets caught in the leg. I sit on the edge of the bed, suddenly hit with the thought that I'm naked and this time he can see me. I look up at him. He reaches his hand through my hair and says, "You're beautiful." Then he takes his boxers off and he's naked too.

I take his hand and pull him down on top of me. I can feel every bit of him pressed onto me as we kiss and he runs his hands along my body.

Gently, he moves his hand down and touches me. I bite my lip to keep from moaning as his fingers slide in and out. I feel the sweetness again, starting to spread over me in waves. But he stops. He reaches down to the side of the bed where his shorts are and pulls out his wallet.

A few moments later, he runs his hand through my hair and his face is close to mine as he starts to push into me. I turn my head toward him, and at first he's leaning on my hair. There's nervous laughter and whispered apologies as we try to keep quiet while we move around. And then he pushes right in and I gasp. Slowly at first, and then faster. The sweet feeling changes to something deeper that builds and builds. I dig my fingers into his shoulders and arch my back.

Chapter 38

I wake up with my face against the wall, and I think for a moment that I'm trapped in some sort of box. Then I remember that Jamie's in my bed. With some effort, I turn around so I'm on my back. I look at his face. His eyelids are fluttering, and I wonder what he's dreaming about. I take in every detail of him. His messy hair, particularly so this morning. His stubble. His mouth hanging open slightly. Despite it all, I feel calm for the first time in months. Nervous, maybe, because I know this changes everything, but I just have this underlying sense that everything has fallen into place.

Then his nose twitches, which makes me snort with laughter, and that in turn wakes him up. He peers at me and frowns.

"'Morning, Joseph," he says through a yawn. He squints at the clock on my bedside table. "Six? What's wrong with you?"

"Shh. You have to sneak back downstairs soon."

He exhales. "Not yet." He pulls me over so that I have my head on his chest.

"Do you know when I realized?" he asked.

"Realized what?"

"I realized I loved you when you woke up really grumpy on my sofa, looking like you'd died."

I dig him in the stomach. "Hey!" But when I rest my head on his chest again, I'm smiling.

"What happens now?"

Jamie shifts under me and breathes in.

The tinkling melody that's been playing in my head since I woke up suddenly goes off key.

"There'll need to be some conversations."

"Yeah."

It's my turn to squirm. I have to tell Dan I can't go to Paris anymore. I get a pang of disappointment as the image of us running for the train fades. We were going to arrive at six in the morning and have coffee on the steps of Notre Dame Cathedral before anyone was awake.

"Can we go somewhere?"

"What do you mean?"

"Can we go away?"

"We have a house in Nice."

"No, not like that. I mean just us. And backpacks. And wandering around a city before anyone else is awake."

"I can assure you that I will never wear a 'backpack.'"

We fall silent again.

"Can I take a photo?" he says.

I flinch.

"Not that kind of photo! Our faces. To remember this."

I look up at him.

"You have a sentimental side, then?"

He frowns. "Yes. You bring out the worst in me, Joseph."

He lifts the phone up and angles it toward us.

Our faces. Mine on his bare chest. The edges of the duvet.

When he's sliding out of the bed and putting his clothes on again, I draw the covers up to my chin. I'm still feeling oddly calm.

He sits on the bed to put his socks on. I prop my head up on my hand and watch him. Then I lean over and kiss him on the shoulder. He turns his head, puts his hand on my cheek, and we kiss. The excitement I've felt since I first saw him is now mingled with a surging happiness.

Then I hear the creak of the front gate. I slip out of bed and go to the window, dragging the duvet with me to cover myself up.

I see him walking quickly along the sidewalk. It's a familiar image.

Slowly and unstoppably, doubts start to seep in.

I clench my teeth together, still staring out the window. What if he goes back to Cleo? Dan doesn't know the full extent of what's been going on. Cleo does. Well, a lot of it. She's been watching it happen. She welcomed me into their clique, and then I did everything she asked me not to right in front of her.

The guilt I'm feeling is hollow. I've got nothing to say except sorry.

Chapter 39

I want to stay in bed as long as possible.

I feel like if I do, then the day hasn't really started yet. I don't have to tell anyone about Jamie. I can just think about him. He loves me. Doesn't he? I slide down under the covers and make a sort of cave. It's warm and smells like him.

I drift off to sleep again and when I wake up, I almost inhale my duvet.

I try reading for a bit, but can't focus. I keep reading the same paragraph. I wonder if I could call the house phone and persuade Matthew to bring me food. As I'm picking up my phone, it vibrates with a text from Gabi.

`Check Facebook`

My account has been hacked.

A steady, sick feeling pulses through me as my profile picture loads. It's me and Jamie. The one he took this morning. My head on his chest. The edges of the duvet. Very clearly in bed together.

My mouth feels dry, my body light and dizzy with panic. I don't know what I'm going to find.

Mia Joseph OMG, finally slept with Jamie last night. SO in love ;)
Mia Joseph READ THIS! Miaslutguide.blogspot.com
   Cleo Farah likes this
   Desdemona Katherine Elliot-Fox likes this
   Desdemona Katherine Elliot-Fox wasn't I good? lol

I click the link.

Hey guys!!!
   I'm Mia. And I'm going to tell you how to be a slut. It's easy. Like me!!!
1. Get a job in a place that gives you access to eligible men.
   Or just men. I'm not picky LOL!
   Really, I'm not.
   I went for Radleigh Castle. The men there are rich too, so it gave me the chance to get into their wallets as well as their pants.
2. Start with something less of a challenge, i.e., someone common and dumb.
   I picked Dan David the kitchen boy.
   (Warning: simpleminded boys like these can get a little attached—use them for a couple of weeks and they'll be ~~making you picnics and inviting you to Paris~~ acting like a total stalker.)

186

3. Select your target. If you have a deluded opinion of your own hotness, like I do, then you'll aim high. Like your employer's son.

That's right, I went there!!! MegaLOLZ

4. Show him that you're ~~desperate~~ eager. It's a technique I like to call "slutting around being a slut." Luckily, you don't need a brain for this, just the willingness to get off with girls, get naked in his swimming pool, and basically wave your vagina around until you get some attention.

5. Be willing to believe anything.

Some examples:

That his sister has passed out and he needs your help. (Can't believe I fell for that!!)

That caring for his sister means there's a sweet side to him (facepalm!)

That he is in love with you.

6. You win! You've had sex with him. Yaaaaayy. Sadly it didn't mean anything and you won't hear from him again, but whatev, you've still succeeded in being a total slut.

P.S. It never does any harm to circulate a few naked pics. Sorry, I mean for "your ex-boyfriend to send them around without your knowledge." ;)

I hold my breath, waiting to see the photo, but the page ends there. He must have really deleted the picture.

This is Cleo. I know it. But Jamie must have sent her the photo.

All the progress, all the things that have made me feel

good or worth something since Kieran, all the things I'd piled up into a tower inside to make me feel strong, sway and come crashing to the ground. I'm back where I was three months ago. No control.

I click back onto my wall and start deleting the statuses and links to the blog. But then I notice some notifications popping up. A screenshot of my wall and the link to the blog have been posted on all my friends' walls.

Chapter 40

I don't really process what's going on. It's like I'm drifting through different scenes with the sound turned down. I've got missed calls from Radleigh, but I don't call back. I can't face work, I think.

But the thought of Radleigh, of Jamie and Cleo hidden away and protected, stirs something.

Soon I'm marching along the river. I don't know what I'm going to do or say. But I want them to feel...something.

It's like time skips forward. I'm standing right outside the castle. Staring up and scanning the windows. I think I'm looking for a sign that anything has changed here. That the lives of the people who live here have been affected in any way. I think I see faces at one of the windows, but when I try to look again, the windows flash back sunlight at me.

"Mia." There's a note of surprise in Julia's voice. "Did you not get my message?"

I shake my head. I'm still trying to look at the windows, but I hear something about going to her office and follow her inside.

On her desk is a printout of the blog.

A short, humiliating conversation follows. I look past Julia and out the window behind her. Jamie doesn't appear at it this time.

I walk back out past the receptionist. I think she *tsk*ed at me.

They're standing at the top of the steps at the front of the house, outside the huge front doors. Jamie, Cleo, and Dezzie.

I stare at them. My face is ghostly white and my hair wild, but I don't care. At least I feel something. Cleo's expression is shining. Triumphant. But Jamie's...

He looks guilty.

I turn my back on them, but feel their eyes boring into me. I hear footsteps, but I don't look back. They quicken, and a few dislodged pieces of gravel bounce past me. I'm nearly at the end of the central path when Jamie skids into view. He stands there blocking my way.

"Mia, wait." He's grinning, but his eyebrows are arched together in a worried frown.

I look at him dully. I still feel numb. "What?"

"I didn't..."

"You didn't what? Pretend your sister was sick?"

His mouth twitches. Nothing comes out.

"Send that picture of us to Cleo?"

No answer.

"Say you loved me so you could sleep with me?"

His eyes meet mine then. Like he's reaching out or trying to send a message. But still he can't speak.

190

"Well done." My voice is coming out monotone. "You win."

I push past him. I'm hit with the smell of damp earth as I start down the path away from the grounds and into the nature preserve Dan took me to. I breathe in deeply and savor it. It smells real. I start walking more quickly, because I think that real feelings are starting to break through the numbness.

I just want to escape. For some reason I'm reminded of when Gabi and I were younger and we used to play a game where you knock on people's doors and run away. One time Gabi got chased up a tree by a woman with a broom. Since then she's always maintained that going up a tree is the best thing to do when in danger, leading to the unfortunate *Hunger Games* incident when she stood up in the cinema, pointed at the screen, and shouted, "SEE?"

I'm deep into the nature preserve now. Jamie didn't follow me. I walk toward a big tree and consider climbing up it for a while. I'd rather there was a woman with a broom chasing me than have this horrible feeling all around me.

I stand with my back against the tree, slide down, and sit there.

Chapter 41

Uneven bits of tree bark are digging into my back. I don't move, though. I've been sitting in the same position with my eyes fixed on my phone screen since I texted Dan to meet.

The snap of a twig makes me look up, and I can see a distant figure with hands in his pockets and wearing a rugby shirt. He's got his head down.

I narrow my eyes, as if I'll be able to tell from here what he's thinking. If he knows. Dan doesn't have a Facebook page.

I get to my feet and he sees me. His head goes down again, but he changes direction toward me.

I watch his sneakers scuffing the ground as he walks. I realize that they're only a few yards away and they've stopped. He's standing there in front of me while I stare at his feet. I wonder how long I can do this before I have to look at him.

Probably not much longer.

His face is stony. No dimples. His head is tilted back, waiting for an explanation.

I run over my lines. I was going to start with, "I never meant to hurt you." Or was it, "All I can say is I'm sorry"? "Sorry is all that I can say"? All of them start morphing into bad boy-band lyrics in my head, and with all the wild panic in there, there's a sudden danger I might start singing.

Eventually I say, "Thank you for coming," like I'm about to give a talk or something. I should ask him to switch off his cell phone.

"Max told me," he says.

"Dan, I didn't..."

"I know you didn't write it. Doesn't mean it's not true."

"No, I mean, I didn't think. I didn't mean for it..."

"Yeah, you didn't think. And because you didn't think, everyone's laughing at me."

"I'm so, so sorry, Dan."

"It's fine." He stabs the ground with his toe, sending chunks of dirt up into the air. "I just...I don't get people who fool around. Maybe I am 'simpleminded.' It *is* simple, to me. 'Do I like her?' 'Yes.' 'Do I want to spend more time with her?' 'Yes.' 'Do I want to be with her?' 'Yes.' I didn't realize it was so complicated with you."

He ruffles his hair and blows out a long breath. "I really liked you."

The lump in my throat is a huge stone. I feel like I'm going to choke on it.

"I don't know why I made it complicated," I manage.

He shrugs. "You like drama?"

I shake my head. But he continues.

"You just wanted to be part of some exciting love story.

193

Two guys fighting over you. In my head we had a love story, anyway. But I guess you found it too boring."

"No." I finally find my voice. "It was too good. I didn't want to ruin it. You thought I was this perfect person who would never hurt you, and all I could think of was that you wouldn't think that if you knew what I'm really like."

Dan nods. "At least that's honest." He thinks for a moment and then looks up at me through his hair. "Look, Mia, don't go along with what people want. You thought I wanted the perfect girlfriend, so you pretended to be it. I bet you pretended with him, too. Do something you actually want to do."

I fiddle with the sleeves of my top. "It's hard to work out why you want something. When you invited me to Paris, it felt all . . . tied up with being your girlfriend. I knew I wanted to go, but I couldn't figure out why."

He smiles at the floor. "I thought we'd have an adventure. Simple as that."

I watch him walk away. Hands in pockets again. But his stride is lighter. I'm jealous that all he has to do is be hurt. Not be hurt, confused, guilty, and a million other things.

I know he's right. I wanted to please everyone. For them to see me in a certain way. When the whole Kieran thing happened, it was the same. I didn't want to stand up and tell him what I thought of him. I just wanted the whole thing to stay secret. Saying nothing or letting things happen is always easier.

I sit back down against the tree and rest my forehead on my knees. Tears stream down my face until my eyes are sore and dry and my head is aching.

I lift my head up and sniff miserably.

Even if I can't work out what I want or why things happen, there's only one place I need to go.

Chapter 42

Gabi is sitting in a ball on the floor of her room. Her chin is thrust forward and her eyes narrow. I know that face. I edge over to her, and a foot is flung out and catches me on the shin.

"Ow!"

"Why didn't you tell me?"

"I'm sorry. You liked Dan so much."

"I do like Dan, but I love you, you stupid bitch."

I sit down next to her and curl up into a ball too.

"You would have told me not to trust him and that I was being selfish and lots of other stuff that's true."

Gabi tilts her head toward me. "I am very wise."

My eyes fill with tears again, and I try to blink them away. "I'm really sorry, Gabs." My voice wobbles at the end and I bite my lip.

She throws her arm out and grabs me in what turns out

to be more of a headlock than a hug. Then she kisses me forcefully. On the eye.

"Stop feeling sorry for yourself. We'll sort you out."

There's a knock on the door, and a millisecond later Gabi's mom bustles in.

"Mom, it's pointless to knock if you don't wait. Mia might have been naked. She's a slut now."

"Oh, yes, I read your blog." Gabi's mom grins at me. "Very funny, though I'm not sure I really understood it."

I think of protesting, but really I'd rather it was like this.

"Gabi, there's a woman on the phone for you. Julie something?"

Gabi goes downstairs to pick up the phone, and her mom turns to me.

"Are you all right, sweetheart? I was worried you girls had fallen out or something."

"I was...I've been a bit stupid. But hopefully she'll forgive me."

"'Course she will—it's you girls! Come and grab a cup of tea. We're going through Gabi's options for college. I've marked the ones she might like." She waves a brochure. Every other page has a Post-it note on it.

"They all sound so interesting," she says as we head downstairs. "What are you taking?"

I stop, and for a moment can't even remember which options I picked.

"His—"

"Oh, your mom said you were doing something exciting—a trip to Paris? Who's the lucky fella? This one I've been hearing about from Gabi?"

Before I get a chance to answer, Gabi bursts into the kitchen waving her arms.

"O. M. F. G!"

The confirmation e-mail comes through.

THANK YOU FOR CLAIMING YOUR PRIZE.

Two tickets to Paris, including train, a fancy hotel opposite the Gare du Nord, a three-course dinner on the first night, and a bottle of champagne on arrival. All I have to do is arrange the dates.

I print it and fold it inside the card I made. It has a black-and-white picture of the Eiffel Tower on it and a heart drawn on crepe paper. I hope it doesn't look too childish. I write the name on the envelope and go downstairs.

Mom's in her office staring with extreme concentration at her computer. She must be having trouble with a design for work. I walk around behind her. She's playing solitaire.

"Mom?"

She yelps and clicks back onto InDesign. She moves a logo on what looks like a brochure a few fractions of an inch to the left. "Hello!"

I fiddle with the doorknob and take a deep breath.

What's the worst that can happen? She can say no.

I've got to try, though. Do something I want to do.

"I've had this idea..."

The conversation I'd been dreading for months went quite well. The college part was fine. And the going away part. I didn't mention the skydiving.

When I left, she gave me a bear hug. I asked what that was for and she said, "Just have a nice day."

It was the same when I came home the day that the blog went up. Mom's on Facebook, so she'd already seen it. She grabbed me in a hug and muttered, "The little shit."

After a while I said, "Mom, you're squashing my nose," but she didn't let go. Not for a long time.

Chapter 43

My phone buzzes again. I go to pick it up.

"Mia," says Jeff. "Stalin!"

"It might be important." I click on the picture. "She's holding up a snail."

"Pardon?"

I hold the phone out to him. Gabi is holding a snail and making the same "argh" face that she was in the picture of her in front of the Eiffel Tower, outside Notre Dame, in the aquarium, and in the Louvre next to lots of works of art that I am not sure she was allowed to take pictures of.

"Mia. Stalin," Jeff repeats, although I see him fighting off a smile.

I tap a few words on my laptop. One of them is "the."

Gabi and I both changed from school to college to do our A-levels. I'm taking history, French, Spanish, and photography. I still remember Jeff drooling into his

Shredded Wheat with joy when I asked him to help me with my enrollment form and saw I was doing history. He also instigated "study Sundays," where I sit with him in his study for a few hours doing schoolwork while he plans lessons. It's not actually as awful as I pretend it is, which is why I'm sitting in here in the middle of midterm break writing an essay.

I had to start Spanish from scratch, but I think it's going okay. It all feels like it's going somewhere. I want to be able to go to countries and speak to people, not do what Mom does and just speak English at them with a foreign accent.

Jeff is writing a to-do list on his notepad. All the things we need to figure out for the Adventure of a Lifetime in December. Gabi and I are going to New Zealand, where Gabi's cousin lives, staying with her and going on an adventure bus tour. As long as we save up the money in time.

Gabi will be fine, with her new role waitressing at Radleigh Castle "with a view toward becoming involved in events management." She asked me if I minded her doing it, but I obviously wasn't going to stand in the way of Gabi and her perfect job. I'm not sure whether Julia realizes that Gabi sees it as "one step away from planning celebrity parties."

I've got a Saturday job at the bookshop. Luckily, when Julia fired me, she said that "to save mutual embarrassment" my reason for leaving would officially be because the late nights would interfere with schoolwork now that classes were about to start. I wouldn't have enjoyed having to explain in a future interview that I left my last job for inappropriate behavior with the boss's son.

That immediately brings up a mental image of just how inappropriate that behavior was. Jamie above me, our faces close and lips almost touching. My fingers digging into his back.

It feels weirdly distant. Like it wasn't even me. Gabi and I have met all these new people in the last few weeks. We've introduced them to the girls, and it's like we have a new gang. It gave me this weird sense of closure. I told them all what happened over the summer. Completely different to what happened with Kieran, where I shut myself off. It made me realize that real friends just want you to be okay. They don't care if you mess up.

And although what I did wasn't great, at least it was based on feeling something. I'd rather be able to admit I fell in love and acted stupidly than be like Jamie and Cleo, who think it's something to be ashamed of. It makes you the loser in their game.

I do still wonder if it was really all a game to him.

My phone buzzes again. Jeff drops his head into his hands and sighs. This time it's ringing.

"Hello?"

"'Ello? Eez zat Meeyah Johzeef?"

"Gabs, your accent is offensive."

"Shut up, dick!"

"How's la Paree?"

"Omigod—awesome. I've eaten all this crap that I don't know what it is. I flashed the Eiffel Tower—just bra, not tit! This woman screamed! Seriously, Mi, thank you *so* much. It is totally the most amazing present anyone has ever given me."

"No worries. My pleasure."

"Max says hi!"

"Hi, Max!"

"But guess who we've bumped into?"

"Who?"

I hear some rustling and Gabi saying, "You speak to her."

"'Ello? Eez zat Meeyah Johzeef?"

It feels like my heart twists.

"Hi, Dan."

"Hello."

"How's... How is it?"

"Really, really great. I'm off to Germany tomorrow evening, but I'm beginning to think I should just lounge around here writing poems and growing a beard."

He'd look good in a beard. I shouldn't say that. I should probably stop saying suggestive things to men in general.

"I like beards." I hope that doesn't make me sound suggestive. Perhaps a little simple.

"Feel free to come out and see it," he says. I can almost hear him stop and panic. I don't think he meant to just invite me to Paris. Again.

Then I hear more rustling and Gabi saying, "Omigod, omigod." She's grabbed the phone back.

"Mia, you should come out here! For the day!"

"I can't go to Paris for a day! Can you even do that? I'm supposed to be saving—"

"Do it! Do it!"

"I can't! It's ridiculous!"

There's a tap on my shoulder. Jeff has slid his notepad across the table to me. Underneath the list he's written, *Eurostar train does day trips. My treat.*

202

Chapter 44

We keep waving as Gabi and Max, laden with bags because someone let Gabi go shopping, walk under the huge departures board and disappear into the crowds.

There's another hour before my train, so Dan and I are going to find a café to sit in.

My hair is still separated into damp strands from the rain.

It was the most torrential downpour I've ever seen. It started in big drops about five minutes after we left the zoo, and the drops very quickly turned into thick jets of water bombing down from the skies. I quickly put on Jeff's sweater, which he made me wear when I left the house at five in the morning, in a feeble attempt to ward off the sogginess. We were in the middle of a big park that led back to the Metro station and stood there in shock for a moment, unsure whether to carry on or run back to the zoo. Gabi decided for everyone when she turned and ran in the direction of the Metro, shouting, "SAVE YOURSELVES!" We all ran, shouting incoherently, and as we became completely soaked, the shouts became a mixture of hysterical laughter and crying.

I was surprised by Gabi's speed. She has, to my knowledge, never attended a PE class. I also had assumed that if she ran too fast she'd be in danger of being knocked out by her own breasts. But, on the contrary, they seemed to give her momentum as a larger and larger gap opened up between us. Similarly, Max managed to go pretty fast, despite the water having traveled all the way up his baggy jeans, causing them to flap behind him.

I was struggling, mainly because my pumps had filled with water and were falling off my feet. Dan was too, because he had his backpack with him. I caught up with him, gesturing wildly at a tree to suggest we shelter for a bit.

We stood under the tree, panting and wiping the water off our faces. I emptied out one of my shoes and then saw Dan peering at me through dripping hair with an odd expression on his face.

"What?" I said, leaning against the tree to take off the other shoe.

"Nothing," he said. He kept looking at me steadily. His eyes shone warmly, and there was the hint of a smile on his lips. I smiled back at him. At least whatever he was thinking was something good. At the beginning of the day, we'd been so polite and careful around each other, making awkward small talk about the food or the hostel or the trains whenever it was just the two of us. But every so often we'd catch each other's eye or say something that made the other one laugh, and I'd get flashes of when we'd just met, of the excited thrill each time we shared a joke. Standing with him under the tree, that happy, crackly feeling surged between us. Looking out at the nearby lake, with the rain bouncing off it, I thought how ridiculously cheesy it would be if we kissed right now.

One of the branches above us must have moved, because a stream of water dropped through, directly onto Dan's head.

"Run again?" said Dan, and I nodded. "Okay, three, two, one!"

On the Metro, people kept their distance, which was fair enough, really, as we looked like a couple of drowned rats.

We got off at Temple and made a dash from the Metro steps to the nearest bar. We'd agreed that when we got somewhere vaguely warm, we'd put on some dry clothes from Dan's bag. Jeff's sweater was so wet that it was practically molded to my skin, and I couldn't wait to take it off. I lifted it up above my head and felt a bit more of a breeze than I'd been expecting. I stopped.

"I'm flashing you, aren't I?"

Dan said, "Umm," in a noncommittal way, and I felt him peel my T-shirt back down. I struggled out of the sweater.

"I'll go and change in the bathroom."

"Cool," Dan said quickly, holding out a top. On my way to find the restroom, an old man gave me an approving nod. Well, at least someone enjoyed getting an eyeful of my bra.

A few minutes later, we both sat at the window looking out at the rain and drinking hot chocolates.

"What an adventure!" I said. "I'm so jealous you're out doing stuff like this while I'm doing homework."

"Seriously? You've come out here for one day and nearly drowned!"

"But if I had to drown anywhere, I'd like it to be Paris."

205

He smiled. "We could try drowning you in some other European cities and see which one's your favorite."

"I'd like that."

There was a pause, and both of us drank from our cups instead of speaking. I realized too late that I'd finished mine already, so ended up doing a very bad mime of drinking.

Then we were interrupted by a face in the window. It looked like some sort of sea monster. It turned out that Gabi had tried to fend off the rain by holding a newspaper over her head, but the paper had disintegrated and molded to her hair.

"I've given up," she said as she sat down. "Max is totally pissed off, though. His hat sank."

Chapter 45

I suddenly snort with laughter, making Dan jump.

"Sorry. I was just thinking about Max and his sunken hat."

He'd put the hat on the table and sat there looking at it mournfully while it curved sadly inward from the top. Then he'd tried drying it on a radiator and gotten even more annoyed when it seemed to be drying in its collapsed state.

Dan grins. "Oh, Max."

We're at a café aross the street from the Gare du Nord. Every so often one of us looks up at the clock on the wall as the time for my train gets closer and closer.

"How have fifteen minutes gone by?" exclaims Dan. "I swear I looked at the clock only a minute ago."

"I don't want to go home," I say childishly.

"Time for one more," says Dan. "My turn."

He goes up to the bar. Outside dusk is setting in; the air

is cool and fresh after the downpour, and the busy streets with people sitting outside chatting are creating an exciting buzz. I look up at him waiting to be served, frowning in concentration at one of the menus and probably seeing how much of it he can read. I remember that I'm still wearing his rugby shirt and should probably give it back, considering he's going to be away for a while. He's off to Germany, and then Eastern Europe next. He traveled around Spain first. He said he didn't want to do Paris at first, after all our planning, but he saw a train when he was in Madrid and thought he might as well come and see the place.

The collar of the rugby shirt is sticking up and is just brushing my nose when I turn to look at Dan. I breathe in his smell. Warm, fresh, and with a hint of honey, I think. Or perhaps that's how it makes me feel. It's a nice, glowing feeling, like honey drizzling off a spoon.

It feels like friendship.

The clock on the wall chimes to mark eight o'clock.

I take off the rugby shirt and leave it nicely folded on top of Dan's bag. I'm a little cold, but I'm sure it will be warm on the train.

Sitting back down, I see my phone, which is on the table, light up.

There's no name, but I know the number. It's pointless, really, to delete someone from your contacts when you know their number anyway. I sit there, looking at the unread message.

I look up at Dan. He's picking up Diet Cokes from the bar and gives me a friendly nod.

My heart is thudding as I pick up the phone. Read or delete?

I click OPTIONS, and my thumb hovers over the delete button. I haven't spoken to him since I saw him outside Radleigh Castle. I've had missed calls, but I've never returned them. I saw a silver car a few times in the parking lot by the college, but I just told myself that there must be more than one person with that car.

I can't resist. I click the message just as Dan sits down.

`Check Facebook x`

Jamie's Guide to Being an Idiot

1. Meet a girl.
2. Realize she makes you laugh and that you feel differently with her than with anyone you've met before. This annoys you. Be rude to her.
3. Try usual techniques. Swimming pool. Wine. *Casablanca*. End up actually enjoying yourself (highly unusual).
4. When it's not working and you are losing her to someone else, be weak. Be persuaded that if you want to get anywhere with her, you'll have to trick her. She would never love the real you. Lie as usual. Allow her to be humiliated because you don't want to admit to anyone else that you love her. Being in love is your version of a dirty little secret.
5. Think about her every day for weeks.

How to Not Be an Idiot
(even if you risk rejection, humiliation, and heartbreak)

1. Turn up at St. Pancras station as she returns from Paris, holding a rose and hoping she forgives you. Make it known that you would be willing to wear a "backpack" and stay in "hostels" and other such uncivilized things.

Really, I'd do anything.

J x

. . .

Jamie Elliot-Fox is toxic.
   Isn't he?

So now I'm here.

The train's moving away. I waved to Dan, and he's heading off to continue his adventure.

I showed him the message, in the interest of honesty. He said he'd only repeat what he said to me before: do something you actually want to do.

For the last few weeks, that's what I've been doing. Choosing, deciding, making my own adventures, not just letting things happen.

One more choice.

Do I believe him?

Well, I've got a few hours to think about it.

Perhaps I should flip a coin.

Acknowledgments

Piccadilly people:

Brenda, for making this happen, expert guidance, and being the first person to meet my characters.

Andrea, for sending me the best books to review, believing I could write, and for a marketing meeting in which we discussed writing *Irresistible* on men's chests.

Anne, for reading the chapters I sent last summer and now being my agent.

Melissa, for my first editing, which has improved my writing more than anything else has done ever, and for spotting Mr. Darcy.

Also Natasha, Margot, and all the other fabulous people who work there!

Family and friend people:

Mum, for instilling in me a love of books and Austen. And just for everything.

Dad, for instilling in me a sense of humor. And for advising me on vintage port.

Edd—otherwise known as "the next Roald Dahl"—for his editorial eye and sarcasm.

Suzy, who is more like a friend than a dog (barely), for encouraging me to write and for many hilarious escapades. Together, we're better by far.

Celia, Emily, Han the Man, Laura, Lorna, Lizzie, Nadia, and Matt. Terribly funny ladies and man. Thank you for all your support in my recent months of being a small author person, and in the years before when I was just a small person.

The admin team at the *Nature* science journal (plus Claire, Tanye, and Haslet), for making my day job hilarious.

Author people (Friends with pens):

Non Pratt, for letting me talk about "bad boys" over a beer, for reading both the book and my crazy e-mails, and for general awesomeness.

Sally Prue, who is *Irresistible*'s official Great-Aunt.

Reader people:

This is YOU. Thank you so much for reading!